M

D0097811

RAWN

THE SWEDISH CAVALIER

THE SWEDISH CAVALIER

Leo Perutz

*Translated from the German
by John Brownjohn*

Arcade Publishing • New York

FIRST NORTH AMERICAN EDITION 1993

First published in Austria in 1936 under the title *Der schwedische Reiter*

The characters and events in this book are fictitious. Any similarity to real
persons, living or dead, is coincidental and not intended by the author.

Library of Congress Cataloging-in-Publication Data

Perutz, Leo, 1882–1957.
    [Schwedische Reiter. English]
    The swedish cavalier / Leo Perutz ; translated from the
German by John Brownjohn.
        p.   cm.
    ISBN 1–55970–170–6
    I. Title.
PT2631.E5S3513   1993
833' .912 — dc20   93–12023

Published in the United States of America by Arcade Publishing, Inc.,
New York, by arrangement with HarperCollins Publishers
Distributed by Little, Brown and Company

10 9   8 7 6 5 4 3 2 1

BP

PRINTED IN THE UNITED STATES OF AMERICA

Foreword

Maria Christine, née von Tornefeld, formerly von Rantzau, subsequently married to the Danish privy councillor and envoy extraordinary Reinhold Michael von Blohme, was a much-admired beauty in her youth. Half-way through the eighteenth century, when she was in her fifties, she wrote her memoirs. This brief work, which she entitled *The Colourful and Richly Populated Tapestry of My Life*, did not appear in print until the beginning of the nineteenth century, several decades after her death, when one of her grandchildren published it for the benefit of a small circle of readers.

The book was not wholly undeserving of its ambitious title, given that its author had seen a good deal of the world in turbulent times. She accompanied her second husband, the Danish ambassador, on all his travels, even to the extent of visiting Isfahan and the court of the notorious Nadir Shah. Her memoirs contain many passages of interest to the modern reader. One of the early chapters gives a graphic account of the expulsion of Protestant peasants from the archbishopric of Salzburg. In a later chapter the author relates how the copyists of Constantinople, deprived of their livelihood by the introduction of a printing press, rioted in the streets. She vividly describes the activities of the faith healers of Tallinn and the violent suppression of that fanatical religious sect. At Herculaneum, to cite her own words, she viewed the first "subterranean discoveries of statues and bas-reliefs sculpted in marble" – not that she grasped the significance of the said finds – and in Paris she rode in a carriage that covered eleven-and-a-half French miles in just under two hours "without horses, solely by means of its own internal momentum".

Maria Christine von Blohme was acquainted with some of the leading intellectuals of her century. Crébillon the Younger, whose mistress she may briefly have been, she met at a masked ball in Paris. She conversed at great length with Voltaire during a masonic function at Lunéville and met him again in Paris some years later, on the day of his admission to the Académie. Also among her friends were a number of scientists such as René de Réaumur and Herr von Muschenbroeck, the experimental physicist who invented the Leyden jar, and there is a certain charm about the story of her encounter with "the celebrated *Kapellmeister* from Leipzig, Herr Bach", whom she heard play the organ in the Heiligen-Geist-Kirche at Potsdam in May 1741.

What makes the strongest impression on the reader, however, is that part of her memoirs in which Maria Christine von Blohme recalls the father she lost at an early age – the father whom she refers to as "the Swedish cavalier" and speaks of with rapturous, almost lyrical affection. His disappearance from her life and the singular and mysterious circumstances surrounding that tragic event cast a shadow over her girlhood.

Maria Christine states that she first saw the light at Klein-roop, her parents' Silesian manor house, and that all the local nobility forgathered there to celebrate her birth. She preserved only a vague recollection of her father, the "Swedish cavalier". "He had frightening eyes," she writes, "but, when he looked at me, it was as if the heavens had opened."

When she was six or a little older, her father left his estate to serve "under the baneful banner of Charles XII", the Swedish king who was famed throughout the contemporary world. "My father came of Swedish stock," she writes, "and all my mother's pleas and lamentations failed to dissuade him."

Before he rode off, however, Maria Christine surreptitiously sewed a little sachet of salt and soil into the lining of his coat. This she did on the advice of one of his two grooms, who had commended it to her as a proven and infallible means of sealing the bond between two people for ever. More will be said of Herr von Tornefeld's grooms at a later stage. Maria Christine

vi

relates that they taught her to swear and play the jew's harp, but that the latter skill had been of scant use to her in adult life.

One night some weeks after her father had gone off to join the Swedish army, the little girl was roused by a tapping on her bedroom window. Her first thought was that it must be "Herod, a kind of legendary or ghostly king" who often haunted her nightmares, but it was her father. She was unsurprised, having known that he would come perforce, compelled to do so by the salt and soil secreted in his coat.

Whispered questions and words of endearment were exchanged. Then they both fell silent and he cupped her face between his hands. She wept a little, partly from joy at their reunion, but also because he told her that he must go away again.

Her father stayed for barely a quarter of an hour, then vanished into the night.

He returned, but always under cover of darkness. Sometimes she awoke even before he tapped on the window. Sometimes he would come two nights in succession, but it might be another four or five nights before he came again, and his visits never lasted longer than a quarter of an hour.

And so it went on for months. In retrospect, Maria Christine found it hard to explain why she should have kept her father's visits from everyone including her mother. She thought it possible that "the Swedish cavalier" had sworn her to secrecy, but she may also have feared that no one would believe her – that people would laugh her to scorn and dismiss her nocturnal experiences as dreams or figments of the imagination.

During the very period when "the Swedish cavalier" was appearing outside Maria Christine's window at dead of night, news of his rapid advancement within the Swedish army was transmitted by couriers from the army in Russia, who paused to change horses at Kleinroop Manor.

His bravery had brought him to the king's notice and earned him a captaincy in the Westgöta Cavalry. He had since been appointed colonel of the Småland Dragoons. His dash and

ſ

daring in that capacity had assured the Swedish forces of victory at Golskva, after which battle the king had, in the presence of the entire army, kissed him on both cheeks.

It saddened Maria Christine's mother that "her dearest love and confidant should not have informed her *par écrit*" how he was faring in the Swedish army. "However," she said, "doubtless he finds it impossible, while in the field, to write so much as a single line."

Then came a summer's day, a day in July, which imprinted itself for ever on little Maria Christine's memory.

"It was about noon," she wrote forty years later. "We were standing in the garden, my mother and I, at the spot where a statue of a little heathen god lay toppled in the grass amid raspberry bushes and dog-roses. My mother, who wore a gown of lavender blue, was scolding the cat for having robbed a bird's nest, but the cat sought to play with her and arched its back so comically that she could not forbear to laugh. Just then we learned that a Swedish courier was in the courtyard.

"My mother hurried off in quest of news and did not return to the garden. Within the hour, however, all the folk on our estate were talking of a great battle at Poltava in which the Swedes had been defeated and their king put to flight. Then they told me that I was fatherless. Herr Christian van Tornefeld, my father, had fallen at the very outset of the battle, unhorsed by a musket ball, and had been buried three weeks before.

"This I could not believe, for it was but two days since he had tapped at my window and spoken with me.

"Late that afternoon my mother sent for me. I found her in the 'Long Room'. She was no longer wearing her gown of lavender blue, and I never saw her attired otherwise than in widow's weeds from that day forward.

"She took me in her arms and kissed me, unable to speak at first. Then she said, in a tearful voice, 'Child, your father has fallen in the Swedish War. He will never return. Join your hands and say a Paternoster for his departed soul.'

"I shook my head. How could I pray for my father's soul

when I knew that he was still alive? 'He *will* return,' I said.

"My mother's eyes filled anew with tears. 'He will never return,' she sobbed. 'He is in Heaven. Now join your hands and do your filial duty: say a Paternoster for your father's soul.'

"Not wishing to aggravate her sorrow by disobeying her, I prayed, but not for the soul of a father who was still alive. I had caught sight of a funeral procession coming down the highroad. The coffin reposed on an open cart, and the dead man's sole attendants were the waggoner, who was whipping his horse along, and an elderly priest.

"It was for this poor man, who may well have been some old vagrant on his way to burial, that I said a Paternoster, entreating God to grant him eternal salvation."

Maria Christine von Blohme concludes her account thus: "But my father, 'the Swedish cavalier', never returned. Never again did his gentle tapping rouse me from my slumbers. As to how he could have fought and fallen in the service of Sweden and, at the same time, have so often entered our garden at night and spoken with me, and why, if he had not been killed, he never returned to tap at my window, that circumstance has remained a dark, dolorous, and unfathomable mystery throughout my life."

What follows is the story of "the Swedish cavalier".

It is the story of two men who met in a farmer's barn on a bitter winter's day early in the year 1701. Thereafter, having struck up a friendship, they trudged on together along the highroad that led from Oppeln, through the snow-clad Silesian countryside, to Poland.

THE SWEDISH CAVALIER

PART ONE

The Thief

THEY HAD SPENT the day in hiding, but now that darkness had fallen they were making their way through a sparse pine forest. Both had good reason to steer clear of people and remain unobserved. One was a vagabond and thief who had cheated the gallows, the other a deserter.

The thief, known locally as "the Fowl-Filcher", endured the discomforts of their night march with ease, for he had gone cold and hungry every winter of his life. His companion, Christian von Tornefeld, was in wretched spirits. He was a year or two younger – almost a boy. The previous day, while they were lying hidden beneath a pile of rush mats in a farmhouse attic, he had boasted of his courage and fantasised about the fame and fortune in store for him. He claimed to have a cousin on his mother's side who owned an estate in the neighbourhood. This cousin would be sure to take him in and provide him with all he needed to get him into Poland: money and clothing, arms and a horse. Once he crossed the border, all would be well. He'd had enough of serving in foreign armies. His father had left Sweden because the king's ministers had deprived him of his crown lands and made a poor man of him, but he, Christian von Tornefeld, had always remained a Swede at heart. Where did he belong, if not in the Swedish army? He hoped to distinguish himself in the eyes of young King Charles, whom God had sent to punish the great for their perfidy. Charles had been only seventeen when he won his world-famous victory at Narva. Yes indeed, Christian von Tornefeld declared: war was a fine thing provided a man had the right brand of courage and knew how to put it to good use.

The thief had made no comment on this. In his days as a farmhand in Pomerania he had earned eight thalers a year and been compelled to surrender six of them in taxes to the Swedish Crown. As he saw it, kings were sent to earth by the Devil, to trample and oppress the common man. He did not prick up his ears until Christian von Tornefeld began to speak of his all-powerful "arcanum", a thing that would commend him to His Majesty's precious and most noble person. The thief thought he knew what such an arcanum must be: a piece of sacred parchment bearing words in Latin and Hebrew that would ward off all ills. He himself had once possessed one and would carry it in his pocket when haunting fairs and markets in quest of a dishonest living, but someone had talked him into selling it for a counterfeit florin. The money was long gone and his luck had turned sour.

Now that they were trudging through the snowy pine woods, their faces lashed by a storm wind laden with hail, Christian von Tornefeld had ceased to speak of war, his courage, and the King of Sweden. He toiled along with his head down, whimpering softly whenever he stumbled over a root. He was hungry. His only nourishment in recent days had been a few turnips and beechnuts grubbed out of the frozen ground. Even worse than his hunger, however, was the cold. Tornefeld's cheeks resembled a deflated bagpipe, his fingers were blue and stiff, and his ears hurt terribly under the scarf wound round his head. His thoughts, as he tottered along through the blizzard, were not of his future prowess in battle but of thick gloves and boots lined with hareskin, and of a makeshift bed of deep straw and horse blankets with a warm stove very close at hand.

It was daybreak by the time they left the forest behind them. Field, pasture and wasteland were covered with a thin layer of snow. Black grouse whirred overhead in the pallid morning light. Isolated birch trees loomed up, their branches dishevelled by the gale, and a white wall of swirling, billowing mist veiled the eastern horizon. Whatever lay beyond it – villages, farmsteads, moorland, ploughland, forest – was hidden from view.

The thief looked about him for some place where they could lie low during the day, but there was nothing to be seen: no house, no barn, not even a ditch or sheltered spot among trees and bushes. He did, however, catch sight of something else and knelt down for a closer look.

A patch of trampled snow and ashes showed where several horsemen had dismounted and bivouacked. From the marks left by carbine butts and entrenching tools, the thief's practised eye deduced that the men who had warmed themselves at the fire were dragoons. Four of them had ridden north and three east.

So a patrol had passed this way. In search of whom? Still on his knees, the thief glanced at his companion, who was sitting huddled on a milestone beside the road, shivering with cold. He looked so disconsolate that the thief knew he must say nothing about the dragoons or the youngster would lose heart completely.

Christian von Tornefeld sensed the older man's gaze upon him. He opened his eyes and rubbed his freezing hands.

"What have you found in the snow?" he demanded in a fretful tone. "If you've found a turnip or a cabbage stalk you must share it with me – that was our agreement. Didn't we promise to help each other and share and share alike? Once I reach my cousin's estate –"

"I've found nothing, God save you," the thief broke in. "How could I have found a turnip in a field sown with winter wheat? I wished to examine the soil, nothing more."

They spoke Swedish together, for the thief hailed from Pomerania and had worked as a farmhand on a Swedish land-owner's estate. He scraped away some snow and picked up a handful of earth, which he crumbled between his fingers.

"It's good soil," he said as he walked on, "red soil such as God used to create Adam. It ought to yield two score bushels to every one of seed-corn."

The farmhand had reawakened in him. Having followed the plough as a lad, he knew how land should be treated.

"Two score bushels," he repeated, "but in my opinion the lord that owns this land employs a bad bailiff and neglectful farmhands. What goes on here, I ask myself? Why such wretched husbandry? They began the winter sowing far too late. Then came a frost and the harrowing had to wait. What's more, the wheat is frozen in the soil."

There was no one at hand to hear. Tornefeld was shuffling along behind, groaning at every footsore step.

"Good ploughmen and harrowers and sowers aren't hard to come by hereabouts," the thief pursued. "I suspect his lordship saves on wages – he hires cheap hands who aren't worth their keep. Any field used for winter sowing should be higher in the middle, so that the rain drains off down the furrows. The ploughman failed to heed that golden rule. He has ruined this field for years to come – it'll be thick with weeds. Here, on the other hand, he has ploughed too deep and turned up poor soil, do you see?"

Tornefeld neither saw nor heard anything. He couldn't fathom the necessity for trudging onward, ever onward. It was broad daylight and time to rest, but still they continued on their endless way.

"His lordship's shepherd is cheating him too," grumbled the thief. "I've seen all kinds of dressing on these fields – wood ash, marl, shavings, garden compost – but not a smidgen of sheep dung. Sheep dung is good, and of benefit to any field, but I suspect that the shepherd sells it on his own account."

And he began to speculate on the nature of the nobleman who employed such lazy, neglectful and dishonest workers.

"He must be as old as Methuselah," he said, "a gout-ridden codger who cannot walk properly and has no inkling of what goes on in his fields. He spends the whole day sitting beside a warm stove, smoking his pipe and rubbing his legs with onion juice. He believes what his farmhands tell him – that's why they cheat him so outrageously."

All this was lost on Tornefeld, who gathered only that his companion had at long last spoken of a warm stove. He was

8

so convinced that he would soon be in a well-heated room that his brain fell prey to hallucinations.

"Today is Martinmas," he mumbled. "In Germany they eat and drink all day long at Martinmas. Smoking stoves, bubbling saucepans, bake-ovens full of pumpernickel. The farmer will welcome us as soon as we walk in – he'll give us the choicest cuts off the goose, and we'll wash them down with a mug of Magdeburg ale followed by a Rosoglio and Spanish bitters. That's what I call a banquet! Drink up, my friend! Your very good health! God's blessing on our festive board!"

Tornefeld came to a halt, raised the imaginary glass in his hand, and bowed left and right. He slipped in so doing and would have fallen flat on his face had not the thief caught him by the shoulder and held him up.

"Look where you're going and stop dreaming!" he said. "Martinmas is long past. Forward march – don't totter along like an old crone leaning on her stick."

Tornefeld gave a start and recovered his wits. The farmer, the smoking stove, the plateful of goose and mug of Magdeburg ale – all these had vanished: he was standing in open countryside with an icy wind buffeting his face. Misery descended on him once more. Bereft of hope and any prospect of an end to his sufferings, he sank to the ground and lay full length.

"Are you mad?" exclaimed the thief. "Do you mean to lie there? What awaits you if you're caught? The stocks, the gibbet, the iron collar, or the wooden boot, that's what!"

"Leave me be, for pity's sake," groaned Tornefeld. "I can go no further."

"On your feet," the thief insisted. "Do you want to be hanged – do you want to run the gauntlet?"

And he was suddenly overcome with rage at the thought that he had joined forces with someone who could do nothing but whine and dawdle. Had he remained on his own, he would long since have reached a place of safety. It would be the youngster's fault alone if they were captured by the dragoons. He was furious with himself for being such a fool.

9

"Why did you desert your regiment if you're so eager to end on the gallows?" he roared. "You should have got yourself hanged right away. It would have been better for us both."

"I wanted to save my life, that's why I deserted," Tornefeld whimpered softly. "The court martial had sentenced me to death."

"What on earth possessed you to strike your captain? You should have knuckled under and bided your time. You'd still be a musketeer living off the fat of the land. As it is, you're lying here with a long face."

"My captain slandered His Majesty's most noble person," Tornefeld whispered, staring stubbornly into space. "He called him a young rake and an arrogant Balthazar for ever spouting the Gospel to distract attention from his escapades. Only a blackguard would have suffered him to speak of my king in such a way."

"For myself, I'd rather have six blackguards than one fool. What concern is the king of yours?"

"I did my duty as a Swede, a soldier, and a nobleman," said Tornefeld.

The thief had briefly thought of leaving him to lie there and making off on his own. When he heard these words, however, it occurred to him that he, too, had his vagabond's code of honour, and that this prostrate youth, for all his fine speeches, was a nobleman no longer: like himself, Tornefeld now belonged to the great fraternity of the destitute. Unable to abandon the boy without besmirching his own honour, he began to reason with him again.

"Get up, friend, I entreat you. Get up, the dragoons are after us – they're out to capture you. Do you want us both to end on the gallows, for Christ's sake? Think of the provosts, think of the thrashing you'll get! Remember, deserters from the imperial army are flogged nine times around the gibbet before they're hanged!"

Tornefeld struggled to his feet and gazed about him with a bemused expression. The veil of mist in the east had been rent asunder by the wind to disclose a vast tract of countryside.

The thief saw that he was on the right track and nearing his destination.

Before him lay a derelict windmill and, beyond it, reeds and marshes and moorland and hills and gloomy forests. He knew them well, those hills and forests. They formed part of the diocesan estate with its forges and stamp-mill, its quarries, smelting furnaces and limekilns. This was a realm ruled jointly by Prometheus and the arrogant bishop known far and wide as "the Devil's Ambassador". On the horizon the thief fancied he could see tongues of flame darting from the limekilns he had fled not long ago. Fire met the eye at every turn, violet and dusky red and stained black with smoke. That was where the living dead, the thieves and vagrants who had once been his comrades, groaned as they hauled the carts to which they were chained. They had escaped the gallows and ended in hell. As he himself had once done, they spent their days breaking stones bare-handed in the bishop's quarries, stone after stone for a term of nine long years. They raked glowing slag from the furnaces before whose fiery mouths they stood day and night in the cramped wooden huts they called "coffins". The flames seared their cheeks and brows, but they no longer felt the heat. All they felt were the whips with which they were driven to work by the bishop's bailiff and his minions.

Such was the place to which the thief aspired to return. It was his last resort and refuge, for there were more gallows than church towers in this part of the world, and he knew that the hemp for the rope that should have hanged him had already been heckled and broken.

He turned away, and his eye fell on the mill. It had stood there deserted for years, the door bolted, the shutters closed. The miller was dead. It was said locally that he had hanged himself because the bishop's bailiff had distrained his mill, donkey and sacks of flour. Now, however, the thief perceived that the sails were turning. He could hear the axle of the great crab creaking and see smoke rising from the chimney of the miller's house.

There was a story current in the neighbourhood. The peasants whispered that the miller left his grave once a year and worked his mill for the space of a night in order to repay a pfennig of his debt to the bishop. The thief had heard this story but knew that it was idle talk. The dead never left their graves. Besides, it was daytime now, not night-time. If the sails were turning in the wintry sunlight, it could only mean that the mill had acquired a new owner.

The thief rubbed his hands and squared his shoulders.

"From the look of it," he said, "we shall have a roof over our heads today."

"All I want," Tornefeld muttered, "is a morsel of bread and a bale of straw."

His companion laughed.

"What were you expecting," he scoffed, "a feather bed with silken curtains? A French *potage*, perhaps, with cakes and Hungarian wine to follow?"

Although the door was unlocked, the miller was nowhere to be seen, neither in his parlour nor in his bedchamber. They even looked for him in the attic, but to no avail. The mill was likewise deserted, yet someone had to be living in the house: a small fire of logs was burning in the stove, and on the table stood a plate of bread and sausage and a pitcher of small beer.

The thief looked about him suspiciously. Being a connoisseur of human nature, he realised that the table had not been laid for folk without a coin in their pockets. He would have preferred to take the bread and sausage and slink off, but Tornefeld, now that he was in a warm room, had recovered his spirits in full. He seated himself at the table, knife in hand, as if the miller had smoked and fried the sausage for his personal benefit.

"Eat and drink, my friend," he said. "You've never been more honourably treated in your life. I'll pay for whatever we consume. A toast, my friend! Your very good health and that of all gallant soldiers! Vivat Carolus Rex! Tell me, are you a Lutheran?"

"Lutheran or Papist as the world pleases," the thief replied, tucking into the sausage. "Whenever I see shrines and crucifixes beside the road I sing out an 'Ave Maria gratia plena' to all who come my way. When I'm in Lutheran territory, I say a Paternoster."

"That won't do," said Tornefeld, and stretched his legs beneath the table. "No man can be two things at once. Persist in that vein and you'll be damned to all eternity. I myself am of the Protestant persuasion – I scorn the Pope and his precepts. Charles of Sweden is the shield and buckler of all Lutherans. Join me in a toast to his health and the death of all his enemies!"

He raised his tankard of ale and drained it.

"The Elector of Saxony has allied himself against Charles with the Muscovite Tsar. I find that laughable. It's as if an ox and a billy-goat had conspired to vanquish a noble stag. Fall to, my friend – enjoy your meal! I'm landlord and cook, waiter and potboy all in one. The cuisine could be better, I grant you. I wouldn't say no to an omelette or a morsel of roast beef. My belly's crying out for something hot."

"But you didn't despise cold fare yesterday," the thief twitted him. "No one could have grubbed up frozen turnips more eagerly than you."

"Ah yes, my friend," said Tornefeld, "they were dreadful days and indescribable hardships – I never thought I'd survive them. I could already see my funeral procession, candles, wreaths, pall-bearers, coffin, and all. Well, I'm still alive, thank God. I've a sure defence against Death's scythe, and in two weeks' time I'll be manning the trenches beside my king."

He patted the pocket in which he kept his "arcanum", as he called it, then pursed his lips and proceeded to whistle a sarabande, beating time on the table with his fingers.

The thief felt a renewed hatred for this aristocratic youth who had so lately sprawled, wretched and despairing, in the snow. He had brought Tornefeld thus far with the utmost difficulty, yet now the boy sat whistling as if every street were too narrow for him and the world itself too small. A living

13

death among the living dead in the bishop's infernal stamp-mill and smeltery – that was the most he himself could hope for, whereas this youngster was free to go forth, armed with his arcanum, in quest of fame and fortune. The thief, who would have given anything to set eyes on Tornefeld's precious arcanum, tried to nettle him into showing it.

"Don't take this amiss, young friend," he said, "but you're setting off for the war like someone going to a country fair. Why not thresh a farmer's corn and sweep out his stables instead? War is hard fare, believe me. To chew it, a man needs sharper teeth than yours."

Tornefeld stopped his whistling and drumming.

"I wouldn't be ashamed to be a farmhand," he replied. "It's an honourable estate – after all, Gideon was threshing wheat when the angel appeared to him – but we Swedish noblemen are born warriors. We're not suited to carting a farmer's corn or sweeping out his stables."

"For all that," said the thief, "I think you're better suited to sitting beside a stove than facing an enemy in battle."

Tornefeld had been about to pour himself another tankard of ale. He kept his temper, but his hand trembled as he replaced the pitcher on the table.

"I shall happily perform any duty proper to an honourable soldier," he retorted. "The Tornefelds have always been soldiers, so why should I skulk beside a stove? My grandfather commanded the Blues at Lützen. He took the field with his king, Gustavus Adolphus, and shielded him with his own body when His Majesty was unhorsed. My father fought in eleven battles and engagements. He lost an arm during the assault on Saverne, but what would you know of Saverne and how things were there? What would you know of the thunder and lightning of battle, the smoke and the screams, the sound of drum and trumpet, the cries of 'Advance!' and 'Retire!', 'Rally!' and 'Charge!'? Nowadays the people of Saverne parch hops and weave carpets. That you may possibly know, but nothing more."

"Yet you quit your company like a coward," said the thief.

"You deserted your regiment in disgrace. I saw you lying in the snow, weeping. You're not fit to be a soldier – you'll never bring yourself to stand guard, dig trenches, charge the enemy, or endure cold and hardship."

Tornefeld remained silent. He sat there with his head bowed, staring into the fire.

"When you hear the drums," the thief pursued, "I suspect you'll fear for your miserable life. You'll look around for a stokehole or a chimney and crawl into it."

"By insulting me," Tornefeld said in a low voice, "you impugn the honour of the Swedish nobility. I won't stand for it."

"Like it or not, it's all one to me," sneered the thief. "I consider all noblemen decadent, and I don't give a fig for their precious honour."

At that, Tornefeld sprang to his feet and stood there, pale with anger and humiliation. For want of any other weapon, he snatched up the pitcher and drew back his arm.

"Not another word," he gasped, "or I'll have your hide."

But the thief had long since armed himself with the bread knife.

"Come on, then," he said with a laugh. "Your threats don't frighten me. Let's see if that arcanum of yours renders you proof against steel. If not, I'll put so many holes in you that . . ."

He broke off. They both lowered their weapons, the one the bread knife and the other the pitcher, suddenly aware that they were not alone.

A man was seated on the bench beside the stove. He had a face like Spanish leather, yellowish and wrinkled, and his sunken eyes resembled two empty walnut shells. He wore a jerkin of red cloth, a broad-brimmed waggoner's hat with a feather in it, and a pair of heavy, knee-length riding boots. And as he sat there in silence with bared teeth and crooked mouth, the other two were overcome with fear. The thief, convinced that this was the dead miller come from Purgatory to see how his mill was faring, surreptitiously crossed himself behind Tornefeld's back. He also invoked Christ's agony, wounds, water and blood in the hope that the miller's ghost would promptly vanish into a cloud of stinking, sulphurous vapour and return to Purgatory, but the man in the red jerkin continued to sit there motionless, staring at them like an owl about to swoop on its prey.

"Where did you spring from?" Tornefeld asked, his teeth chattering. "I didn't see you come in."

"A little old woman brought me in a bucket," the man replied with a low laugh. His voice had the muffled sound of one shovelful of graveyard soil landing on another. "What of you? What are you doing here, eating my bread and drinking my beer. You expect me to say grace for you?"

"He looks as if the Devil's kept him pickled in vinegar for ten years," the thief muttered to himself.

"Hush, he may take offence," Tornefeld whispered hurriedly. Aloud, he said, "Your pardon, sir, but everything's frozen stiff outside and times are so hard that I haven't tasted a morsel of bread for three whole days, so help me God. That's why I sat down at your table uninvited."

"He looks as if a weasel breathed in his face," the thief said softly.

"Uninvited, sir," Tornefeld repeated with a bow, "although I don't have the honour of your acquaintance. However, rest assured that you'll be duly recompensed."

The thief realised that this was no way to converse with a ghost. It also occurred to him that he had used the wrong formula in his haste and confusion. One invoked Christ's blood and wounds against dropsy, smallpox or gangrene, but not to banish evil spirits. Before he could recite the correct spell, the man in the waggoner's hat turned and addressed him.

"From the way you look at me, fellow, you know who I am."

"I know too well who you are," the thief replied in a trembling voice, "and I also know where you hail from. You've come from the House of Limbo, where the windows belch flame and folk bake apples on the windowsills."

16

He had a vision of Purgatory, the fiery abode of souls in need of purification. That was the House of Limbo, but the man in the red jerkin took him to mean the bishop's smelting furnaces and limekilns, from which smoke and tongues of flame rose heavenward day and night.

"I see you don't know me after all," he said. "I'm not one of my lord bishop's smelters, foundrymen or furnacemen."

Snowflakes were whirling outside. The thief took a step toward the window and pointed to the windmill's sails, which now hung motionless.

"It's my belief," he said in a low, halting voice, "that you're the same miller who fled this world with a noose about his neck, and that you now dwell in the fiery abyss."

"Yes, I'm that same miller." The man in the red jerkin rose from the bench beside the stove and fell to pacing up and down. "Yes, I'm he, and it's true that I once, at an evil hour, sought to end my life with a rope, but the bailiff and his minions arrived in time. They cut me down and the surgeon bled me. My life was restored to me. Now I'm a waggoner in the service of His Grace the bishop. I drive back and forth along the highway, bringing my master merchandise from all manner of lands and cities – from Venice and Mechlin, Warsaw and Lyon. And you? What's your trade? Whence do you come and whither are you bound?"

The thief eyed him uneasily as he paced the room, spurs jingling. He felt sure that this long-dead man, who tried to pass for a creature of flesh and blood, knew perfectly well that he was looking at a thief who had spent his young life stealing all that came his way: bacon and eggs, bread and beer, ducks from the pond and nuts off the tree. Rather than speak of his trade, therefore, he levelled a hesitant finger at the gloomy woods in which the forges and the stamp-mill lay.

"That's where I mean to go and earn my bread."

The miller chuckled softly and rubbed his bony hands.

"If that's where you mean to go," he said, "your wish can be speedily granted. His Grace the bishop is a good master. You'll get half a pound of bread in your hand and another half in your soup every day, plus two kreuzers' worth of dripping, gruel for supper, and on Sundays groat sausage and stewed mutton."

The thief shut his eyes. Times were hard. Hot food had crossed his lips only once in the last ten days, and that was when he'd killed and roasted a jackdaw. He drew in his breath as if the meat platter were already on the table before him.

"Stewed mutton," he murmured, "with carraway seeds –"

"With carraway and nutmeg," the miller assured him. "You'll be royally regaled, believe me."

He turned to Tornefeld.

"And you, why do you stand there like a painted saint? Have you lost the use of your tongue? Are you also after an easy life? Is my lord bishop to feed every idler and glutton that comes this way?"

Tornefeld shook his head.

"I shall not be remaining hereabouts," he said. "I intend to cross the frontier."

"The frontier, eh? Have you a mind to sample pepper cakes and Polish brandy at Kielce?"

Tornefeld stood as erect and motionless as if he were already drawn up on parade.

"I mean to serve my liege lord, the King of Sweden."

"The King of Sweden?" exclaimed the miller, and his voice became suddenly shrill. "Oh yes, he's awaiting your advice on how to defeat the Great Cham and the Emperor of China – he's afraid his legs will swell up unless he covers himself in glory. So you mean to seek your fortune in the Swedish army? You'll be given four kreuzers a day to spend on chalk and talcum, boot polish and emery. A soldier's luck is like corn on a poor man's barren plot: it never thrives."

"My mind's made up for all that," said Tornefeld. "I'm off to the Swedish war."

The miller advanced on him as if eager to see the whites of his eyes. The wind continued to howl and the roof beams groaned under their burden of snow, but inside all was still. Nothing could be heard but the three men's breathing.

"You fool!" the miller said at length. "You'll be Death's meat soon unless someone talks some sense into you. One pound of lead makes sixteen bullets, and one of them has already been cast for you. Nowadays, every fool yearns to join the Swedish army, and once he does so he rues it. What have you run away from – the plough, the tailor's yardstick, the cobbler's stool, the quill and inkpot?"

"None of them," Tornefeld replied. "I'm a nobleman. My father and my grandfather spent their lives in the field, and I mean to do likewise."

"Well, well, so you're a nobleman," sneered the miller. "You look more like a scabby cuckoo, you're so tattered and tousled. Do you have a passport and papers?"

"I possess neither passport nor papers," said Tornefeld. "I have nothing but my courage and the will to fight, and I'll stake my soul –"

The miller raised a deprecating hand and lowered it again.

"Keep your soul," he growled, "no one else has need of it. You may, however, be aware that every road is teeming with soldiers tonight – dragoons and musketeers in search of Polish brigands and out to make an end of them. You'll find it hard to cross the frontier without a passport and papers."

"Hard or not," said Tornefeld, "my mind's made up. I'm off to the Swedish war."

"Then go to the Swedish war!" the miller cried in a voice that sounded as strident as an ungreased waggon wheel. "I'll not assist you to an easy life after all. Just pay for your meal and begone!"

Tornefeld was overcome with fear to see him standing there with clawlike hands and bared teeth and eyes that flashed like will-o'-the-wisps. He longed to toss a half-guilder on the table and take to his heels, but his pockets, even if turned inside out, would not have yielded one miserable kreuzer.

He took two paces to the rear and sidled up to the thief.

"Friend," he whispered, "look in your pockets to see if you

can find a guilder or a half-guilder. This skinflint expects me to pay him, and I have no money left."

"Where would I find a guilder?" the thief protested. "It's such an age since I saw one, I can't remember if it's round or square. Didn't I hear you say you'd pay for whatever we ate and drank?"

Tornefeld cast an apprehensive glance at the miller, who had bent over the stove and was poking the fire.

"In that case," he told the thief, "it all depends on you. You must go at once to my cousin at Kleinroop Manor, near the village of Lancken. Inform him that I'm here and ask him to send me money and clothes and a horse."

"I wish you a long and happy life, my friend," said the thief, "but my skin is as precious to me as yours. I've no wish to run into the dragoons, and anyway, what concern of mine is your cousin?"

Tornefeld gazed through the window at the snowstorm, which was growing worse by the minute. The windmill's sails were no longer visible.

"You must go in my place," he insisted. "You'll earn my eternal gratitude. I'm ill, as you can see – I couldn't be more so. It would be the death of me if I had to venture out into the cold."

"You're afraid it might freeze your nose off," jeered the thief. "How often have you boasted of your courage and your eagerness to serve in the Swedish war? You ply me with kind words now – yes, but a minute ago you threatened me with that pitcher. You'd gladly have seen me hanged and broken on the wheel. Whoever goes, it won't be your humble servant."

"Forgive me, friend," Tornefeld pleaded. "I'm sorry – I was only jesting, as God is my witness. I won't disguise the truth from you: I dread neither the dragoons nor the cold, but I don't wish my noble cousin and the demoiselle his daughter to set eyes on me in my present rags and tatters. Go in my place – do so for the sake of brotherly love. Tell him that I shall be honoured to call on him as soon as I look like a gallant

20

soldier once more. You'll be well entertained and generously rewarded for your services."

The thief deliberated. To reach the village of Lancken, which was three miles away, he would have to go back the way they had come. It might be that the ill-tended fields flanking the road belonged to his fellow sufferer's high-born cousin, and he was curious to see the man who allowed himself to be so woefully robbed and cheated by his bailiff, clerks, shepherds, and farmhands.

It would be dangerous, he knew. If he fell into the hands of the dragoons he would be hanged for a surety on one of the gibbets that stood at every crossroads, but he was used to danger. Fate had often presented him with a choice between starvation and the noose. Now that he had resolved to end his vagabondage and surrender his freedom in exchange for a daily dole of bread and a roof above his head, he felt a perverse desire to go out where the keen wind blew and dance one last courante with Death.

"Stay, then, and I'll go," he told Tornefeld. "But will his excellency your cousin deign even to be seen by a person of my humble rank?"

"Any man is worthy of another's consideration," Tornefeld said quickly, fearful lest the thief should change his mind. "Show him this signet ring – then he'll know that I sent you. Be brief and to the point. First, he's to give you some money for me, for I shall have to replenish my purse if I'm to get across the frontier. Secondly, he's to send me a carriage, a warm coat, some shirts, neckerchiefs, red silk stockings –"

"He'll say I stole this," the thief interjected with a dubious glance at the silver signet ring which Tornefeld had just removed from his finger.

"He won't," Tornefeld said firmly. "But if he does, you must prove your bona fides by reminding him of how, in my boyhood, I and the demoiselle his daughter rode downhill in a sleigh and were overturned when the horses bolted. When he hears that, he'll know you come from me. And he's also to send me one coat of flowered brocade and one of satin adorned with ribbons and lace. A braided hat, two black wigs, a silken dressing-gown –"

"What is your cousin's name?" the thief broke in again.

"Christian Heinrich Erasmus von Krechwitz auf Klein-roop," said Tornefeld. "He stood sponsor for me at my christening. And don't forget the two black wigs, one large and one small, and the braided hat, and the alamode coat of satin . . ."

But the thief was already on his way. An icy blast filled the room. The miller straightened up and warmed his hands at the glowing stove.

"Herr Christian von Krechwitz," he murmured. "I knew him well. A stern and masterful man. God rest his soul."

Darkness was falling when the thief reached the village. Although the snow had ceased, the cold was becoming ever more intense and the wind that whistled about his ears was as keen as a knife. The village street was deserted save for a big brown dog roaming among the wretched houses and shacks. A dim glow and the muffled strains of a bagpipe issued from the tavern. Visible at the far end of an avenue of maple trees was the slate roof of Kleinroop Manor, glistening wet where the snow had been melted by the warmth of its chimneys.

While making his way toward the house across the frozen fish pond, the thief could not but think again of the noble lord who employed the worst of all farmhands and suffered them to ruin his land. "Why does this Herr von Krechwitz never leave his house?" he wondered. "He need walk only once across his fields to see the state they're in. He must be blind not to see it, blind or lying ill abed. Perhaps he has the dropsy or spits blood – perhaps he spends the whole day swallowing olive oil, wormwood juice and electuaries. Why does he never visit his fields? Perhaps he's a dreamer and visionary who closets himself in his room, summer and winter, pondering on the appearance of the moon's interior, or on whether more men than women go to heaven. Or isn't he on his estate at all? I'd make a wager with myself, right pocket against left, that he doesn't live here. He lives in the city and devotes his time to fencing, dancing, sitting at the gaming table and serenading the ladies. He lets his workers do as they please and visits his estate only to get money – that's Herr von Krechwitz for you. And when he has collected a hundred thalers he returns to the city and remains there until he has spent the hundred and increased his debts by a few hundred more – yes, that's Herr von Krechwitz for you. Being in debt, he sits there planning how to become rich overnight. I could advise him on that score. The land itself is good: only one hide of wasteland to every three of tilth. If he had it better dressed and sown as it deserves – stubble grain on some fields, early white oats on others, and wheat on the richest soil only – yes, if he had it properly sown and better harrowed and weeded, he'd soon see how standing grain ought to look, stalk after stalk of it. Mark you, he'd also have to discipline his farmhands, keep a sharp eye on his clerk, send his bailiff packing and take matters into his own hands – yes, he'd have to do that instead of living in the city with liveried servants and paying musicians to play below ladies' windows . . ."

The thief's roaming thoughts were abruptly dispelled by a tinkling of bells and the crack of a whip. He leapt aside and crouched down behind a snowdrift.

A sleigh was gliding slowly and ponderously across the fish pond's frozen surface – a creaking, rumbling old sleigh drawn by one emaciated horse, but the torn and faded leather of the door bore vestiges of a nobleman's coat of arms. A lantern on the driver's box lit the face of the man seated in the back, who was wearing an old sheepskin coat. The thief caught a fleeting glimpse of a bulbous nose blue with cold, a sour mouth, and a beard parted in the middle.

He got up from behind the snowdrift and stared after the sleigh, shaking his head.

"So that's Herr von Krechwitz," he muttered to himself. "He's no dreamer or visionary, nor does he look like a man who chases women and gives them presents, far less loses his money at the gaming table. His is the face of someone who's never satisfied and wouldn't lend a three-pfennig piece.

Miserly and ill-natured, that's what he looks, but why doesn't such a stern master contrive to gain his servants' respect?"

The thief pondered this as he walked on, and it was not long before he found a solution to the mystery.

"I have it," he said to himself. "Herr von Krechwitz must have done some evil deed and concealed it from the outside world. No one knows of it save his servants, but they keep mum – that's why he's now in the palm of their hands. Perhaps he murdered his brother for the sake of his inheritance, or poisoned his wife for her money. His servants know this, and he fears they may give him away and bear witness against him. That's why he dares not rid his estate of a single one."

The sleigh drew up outside the manor house gates, which were opened from within. A groom appeared with a lantern. He gave a low, respectful bow, but the man in the sleigh jumped up, snatched the whip from the driver's hand, and began to lay about the groom in a fury.

"You rogue, you polecat's hide!" he bellowed at the top of the voice. "You oaf of a peasant, you unmitigated fool! Why did you send me the worst sleigh and the lamest nag? May the Devil reward you for your pains! No, hold your tongue! I shall have to dose you with an iron spoon to teach you who I am."

The groom simply stood there in an attitude of submission. At length, growing weary, the man in the sleigh dropped the whip. The groom stooped to pick it up, the sleigh disappeared into the courtyard, the gates closed behind it, and darkness and silence returned.

"That's the way, that's the way," the thief muttered, rubbing his hands. "He knows how to treat those scoundrels, and it serves them right. They all merit a thrashing, but if he flogs them like dancing bears for so little reason, why the devil doesn't he take better care of his estate? Why does he let his fields go to ruin and his seed-corn rot in the ground? That I don't understand. No, by God, I don't understand it at all."

He walked on, shaking his head. Although the gates were shut and bolted, his practised eye quickly discerned a spot where he could scale the wall without difficulty. And then, while he was cautiously hauling himself over it, he had another idea which seemed to provide the simplest explanation for Herr von Krechwitz's strange behaviour.

"There are landowners hereabouts who set greater store by their stables and cowsheds than their fields, and wise they are to do so. A cow won't fetch less than nine thalers – indeed, I'd undertake to sell one for ten provided she's a good milker. Counting just the calf, butter and dung, a cow will bring in four reichsthalers a year. Then there are sheep. The sheep has a sharp set of teeth. It needs only a shepherd and some coarse grass on sandy soil, but it will yield a pound-and-a-half of wool per shearing. There's many a man who wishes himself in Herr von Krechwitz's shoes, I'll be bound. He doesn't give a fig for hailstorms or blight or pests such as mice and beetles: he has rented out his ploughland and devoted himself to breeding livestock. Foals, lambs and calves are his source of revenue. Silesian wool is exported to Poland and the Muscovites – even to Persia. Fine wool always fetches a fair price. He knows what he's doing, this Herr von Krechwitz . . ."

While all this was passing through his mind, the thief slid down the wall, landed in the snow, and got to his feet again. The yard was completely deserted. An overturned harrow lay near the entrance, and a pitchfork jutted from the snow. The sleigh was already in the coach house, the horse in its stable. The farmhands had doubtless stopped work for the day and retired to their quarters.

The thief made his way slowly and irresolutely toward the house, only to pause after a few steps. He was in no hurry. Tornefeld could wait another hour for the alamode coat and braided hat and red silk stockings without which he declined to go to war. Yes, Tornefeld could wait – the thief didn't care. Before delivering his message to the lord of the manor he wanted to see the sheep that must surely be celebrated far and wide, even across the frontier in Poland. He wanted to inspect the Spanish breeding rams and see how the ewes were quartered and how their lambs were withstanding the hard winter.

The door of the sheep-shed was locked, but locked doors

presented no obstacle to the thief. Nimble and noiseless as a lynx, he scaled the wall and squeezed through a narrow aperture into the loft. From there he climbed down a ladder into the sheep-shed itself.

So these were Herr von Krechwitz's famous sheep! They looked wretched enough in all conscience: less than three dozen animals housed in a building that could have held a hundred or more – three dozen neglected sheep of which all bore the coarsest wool and many were bloated with poor fodder. As for Spanish breeding rams, there was none to be seen.

The thief took the sheep-shed lantern and went from beast to beast, counting the wethers and rams, yearlings and two-year-olds and ewes.

"No," he said to himself, as indignant as if the sheep had been his own, "his lordship gets no revenues from his flock – he's clearly being robbed. It isn't easy to find an honest shepherd, mark you. All shepherds are rogues – even the best of them get their own lambs suckled by the master's ewes – but this one is the worst of all. Two loads of hay, just as it comes from the meadow, that's all that's needed to get thirty sheep through the winter, yet all I saw in the loft was straw, not a single bale of hay. The shepherd must have sold the fresh grass from the meadows for ready money, and now he's feeding the sheep on coarse-chopped straw. Fodder of that kind is poison to sheep. He's letting the flock go to rack and ruin."

He paused beside one of the beasts and examined it closely.

"This sheep is sick," he said. "It isn't the mange. Perhaps it has lung-worm or wool-rot. That comes of not keeping it dry enough. The shepherd doesn't know that sheep cannot stand the damp. If I were Herr von Krechwitz . . ."

He put the lantern down and opened the animal's mouth.

"Dear God!" he exclaimed in horror. "No, that's not lung-worm. This sheep has an inflammation of the spleen, and the shepherd either doesn't know or doesn't care. He should slaughter it at once, in such a way as to spill no blood, and bury the carcass deep, but he leaves the sick beast with the rest

26

of the flock. And his lordship? His lordship must be far too fond of his creature comforts to visit the sheep-shed, perhaps because he finds the smell distasteful. He shall learn what manner of shepherd he has, though. He shall learn that his sheep-shed harbours splenic fever!"

The thief had seen enough. He stole out as noiselessly as a cat leaving a pigeon-loft. For a while he roamed among the farm buildings enclosing the courtyard, and what he saw convinced him that his lordship was threatened with ruin on every hand.

"His farmhands and their womenfolk are afraid of hard work – they're worthless riff-raff, one and all. The grain is mouldering in the granary and their winter tasks have yet to be completed. They've chopped no wood. Flax should already be dried and broken at this time of year, yet they haven't even pounded it. His lordship employs none but gluttons and drunkards. The master shepherd and his underlings enjoy milk soup and roast meat on workdays, and each has a big mug of ale set before him. Everything here is arsy-versy: the servants live in luxury while their master goes short. Thunder, lightning and hellfire, if only I were Herr von Krechwitz! The look of that cow-shed, too! Cows need fresh litter daily. As for calves, they have to be cosseted like new-born babes, but here . . ."

The door of the cow-shed opened and two men emerged. The thief barely had time to drop to the ground.

One of them appeared to be the bailiff charged with administering the estate, for he was laden like a mule with books of accounts. He had two in one hand and three beneath his arm, a stable lantern in the other hand, an ink-pot in his belt, and a brace of quill pens behind his ear. He stood submissively before the fork-bearded man whose sledge had passed the thief not long before.

"So he's seen the state of the stables," thought the thief, who was hugging the ground and shivering with cold. "Now for another thrashing! He looks as if he means to break the bailiff's neck in a thousand places. If I were to stand up and tell him that the other buildings look worse still, and that one of his sheep has splenic fever . . . Ah, now for it!''

"You must be mad!'' bellowed the fork-bearded man, so loudly that the startled bailiff dropped his ledgers in the snow. "Two hundred guilders? Spare me! Palm Sunday, that's your day – that's when you may show your face, but not before. Two hundred guilders? Where am I to find them, pray? D'you think my purse is a bottomless well? I lent your employer three hundred guilders on the morrow of Passion Sunday and another two hundred and twenty on St Leonard's Day. Money spews from this house like smoke from a chimney.''

He paused to catch his breath, his face empurpled with rage and cold. The bailiff proceeded to plead with him in a piteous voice.

"As Your Excellency knows, the house is full of uninvited guests who expect to see roast meat and wine and omelettes on the table every day. The peasants, too, come pestering us for bread and seed-corn.''

"Tell your employer to sell a few rings and necklaces – they'll fetch some money,'' snapped the fork-bearded man. "Mine is strewn around the countryside. I've made loans far and wide and can't call them in.''

"The rings and necklaces went to the Jew long ago,'' sighed the bailiff. "We've sold the silver tankards and ewers, the coaches, carriages and chaises. We've borrowed the money for the autumn sowing from all and sundry, and we'll have to repay twelve bushels for every ten. My employer thought that Your Excellency, being so kind and generous a godfather –''

"Hell's bells!'' cried the fork-bearded man. "So I'm your employer's kind and generous godfather once more, am I? Perhaps, but where was *I* last year, when they buried your late lamented master? Where was *I* when Kaspar von Tschirnhaus carried his helmet and Peter von Dobschütz supported his shield on the right and Baron von Bibran led his horse? Where was *I* when Georg von Rottkirch carried the escutcheon and Hans Üchtritz auf Tschirna the cross and sword? Where was

28

I when Melchior Bafron supported his shield on the left and the Nostitzes and the Lilgenaus held his shroud in church? I had to lend the money for the velvet horse-cloths, and the banner of red double taffeta, and the preacher, and the wax candles. Two hundred and twenty guilders I lent, and in return I was privileged to sing 'Now lay we him to rest' in the choir. That was the only honour accorded me."

The thief had heard enough. Far from being the lord of the manor, the man with the bulbous nose and the forked beard was a local money-lender – one of the breed that preyed on manorial estates, amassed money for themselves, and begrudged their neighbours a morsel of food and a roof over-head. "For shame!" muttered the thief. "A common money-lender, and I took him for a nobleman. How could my eyes have deceived me so! I must listen carefully, for the pair of them are hatching some crooked scheme. Their heads are as close together as nuts on a cedar tree – they look like Judas plotting with Iscariot."

The Judas of a bailiff shuffled his feet in the snow while the Iscariot of a money-lender noisily blew his nose.

"Convey my respects to your employer," said the money-lender, "and say that Baron von Saltza auf Düsterloh und Pencke declines to lend another thaler or guilder. He requires no orchards or grazing rights as surety, but if your employer were willing to sell Diana and Jason, the mare and the grey-hound, he would give eighty guilders for them. If the mare and the greyhound are not for sale, so be it. Harness up and I'll head for home."

"God have mercy!" sighed the thief. "So he's a nobleman. He styles himself baron and sports a coat of arms, but it doesn't offend his sense of honour to practise common usury. I'm glad I'm not a nobleman of that kind – I'd sooner remain in the gutter."

"Eighty guilders are little enough," the bailiff said. "The dog alone is worth fifty, as Your Excellency must be aware."

"I'll pay eighty guilders, not a kreuzer more," the money-lender declared. "It's a bad bargain, for a saddle-horse and a hound cost more per day in food and upkeep than they profit their owner in a month."

"But these particular beasts *will* be of profit to Your Excellency," the bailiff said slyly, with a bleating laugh. "My employer will have to knock on your door for a sight of Jason and Diana, and that, I know, will be a daily occurrence. My employer will find life unbearable without them."

"You think so?" said Fork-Beard. "Well, if your employer does come knocking at my door, I'll not be inhospitable. Tell your employer that Baron von Saltza resembles the basil in a herb garden: handle it roughly, and it stinks like the deuce and makes the eyes smart; stroke it gently, and it gives off a delicious scent."

"I'll harp on that every day," the bailiff promised. "Make it a hundred and ten guilders, Your Excellency: eighty for my employer and thirty for me. I've always been Your Excellency's faithful servant – I've always had Your Excellency's interests at heart."

"Twenty for you, that's quite enough," said Fork-Beard, whose mood appeared to have undergone a sudden change for the better. The two of them set off for the house while the thief half-rose and brushed the snow from his clothes.

"This is a sorry business," he said to himself. "If every scoundrel on the estate had to wear a bell around his neck, no one would be able to hear himself speak. Poor Herr von Krechwitz! I'll tell him that his sheep-shed's a hotbed of disease, and his bailiff's robbing him, and his godfather's cheating him, and his workfolk are growing fat while he himself grows poorer by the day. He shall learn from my own lips how things stand with him. Whether or not he rewards me with a bowl of beer soup, I'll do it for Christian charity's sake."

He got to his feet. A strange transformation had come over him. Mindful no longer of his errand for Tornefeld, he was now preoccupied with another mission. It seemed to him that he, a thief, was the only honest man on the estate, and as such he had resolved to speak to the lord of the manor.

Ordinarily, when entering a strange house, he would have

crept inside as furtively as a mole invading a flower garden; on this occasion he made straight for the door, erect and fearless for the first time ever. He was an honest man requesting admittance – an honest man with some plain words in store for the lord of the manor.

But, just as he reached the door and was about to knock like anyone devoid of ill intent, it opened abruptly and two dragoons – two mortal enemies of himself and all other vagrants – emerged carrying lanterns and nosebags. At sight of them the thief forgot his honest man's role and felt a resurgence of his old, thievish fears. He took to his heels and ran off round the house, and the dragoons dropped their nosebags and ran after him. "Who's there? Answer!" he heard them call. "Halt or I fire!" But he paid no heed. He had already turned the corner and was running for his life when he heard more voices ahead of him. That stopped him in his tracks.

"Where can I hide?" he gasped. "Where?"

Close to where he was standing the snow had been shovelled together into a mound. He flung himself down, burrowed his way into it, and lay there until the dragoons had gone by. "Where can the fellow be?" he heard them shouting. "Has the Devil carried him off?" At last, when all was quiet again, he cautiously raised his head. There was no sign of the dragoons, but they might reappear at any moment. He extricated himself from the mound of snow, wondering where next to hide. Above him, almost twice the height of a man from the ground, was a window with a broad sill. "If only I could reach that!" he thought. He took a run, leapt for the sill, and managed to catch hold of it. The wood was studded with broken glass and nails which tore his hands to ribbons, but he ignored the pain and hauled himself up. Once on the sill he expertly opened a broken shutter, then thrust his legs through until he felt his feet touch the floor.

It was thus – half-frozen and soaked to the skin, his lungs on fire, his hands bleeding, his limbs trembling with fear, cold, and exhaustion – that the thief first gained access to the house whose master he was to become less than two years hence.

31

The room was filled with lumber of all kinds. For a while the thief simply stood there with no thought in mind save that he was bitterly cold, and that he had, as so often before in his wretched life, escaped the gallows by a hair's-breadth. Yes, but for how long? He must find Herr von Krechwitz and speak with him, but his arch-foes the dragoons were billeted in this house and he risked running into them a second time. No matter. Being both unable and unwilling to retrace his steps, he must find Herr von Krechwitz come what might. He waited for his breathing to subside, then groped his way forward. His eyes having grown accustomed to the gloom, he made out a heavy, iron-bound door ahead of him. It was unlocked and ajar, and from the crack issued a faint, almost imperceptible shaft of reddish light. Its source was neither a candle nor an oil lamp, the thief could tell. There was a fire burning in the stove opposite the door, but that was all: the room was otherwise in darkness. No light meant no people, the thief told himself, for no one willingly sat in the dark. He breathed a quiet sigh of satisfaction. An empty room with a fire in the stove could not have been more welcome to someone so eager to warm himself and dry his clothes.

He stood there listening for another minute, then cautiously pushed open the heavy door and tiptoed over the threshold.

Yes, there was a wood fire burning in the stove. Its faint glow fell on a silver-cabinet standing against the wall, but this was empty. The thief pulled a face, then suddenly remembered that he had not come there to steal.

"It's just as that fellow said," he thought, smiling to himself. "Herr von Krechwitz has sold everything to the Jew – rings and necklaces, silver platters and ewers. He doesn't live too badly for all that . . ."

He snuffed the air. He could smell wine, fresh bread, roast meat. Someone had eaten supper here and left some over for him, the thief. On the table were dishes, platters, glasses, and a pitcher of wine. Where could he be now, the man for whom the table had been laid and the stove lit? The thief surveyed the room. Something lying across a chair caught the light: a sword-blade. Beside the stove stood a lone riding boot. Between the two windows was a bed, and in that bed – the thief caught his breath – in that bed lay a man.

The thief kept his head. He was used to such contingencies, and sneaking through bedrooms without waking their occupants was part of his trade.

Except that the man in the bed was neither asleep nor alone. There were two people lying there, a man and a woman.

The thief didn't stir. The man in the bed must surely be Herr von Krechwitz. His lordship had retired early after wining and dining well, and was now enjoying the company of his beloved wife. Being eager to have a word with him, the thief debated how best to make his presence known and open the conversation.

"God's blessings on this house, sir," he improvised softly, giving a little bow, then went off at a tangent. "My, will he leap out of bed when I tell him of the splenic fever in his sheep-shed! But that can wait. It isn't time yet. First I want to see what the pair of them are up to."

He listened, highly gratified that chance should so soon have guided him to Herr von Krechwitz. Rustling and whispering were all he heard at first. Then came a smothered yawn. The man in the bed sat up and stretched his arms.

Meantime, the thief embarked on another rehearsal of his speech. "Sir," he muttered, "you lie abed in ignorance that there's splenic fever in your sheep-shed. Your farmhands are ne'er-do-wells – they should all be . . ." He broke off. "No! I can't begin like that. That would be like putting my right foot in my left boot. First I must tell him where I come from and who sent me."

"Why do you yawn so?" the girl in the bed said suddenly. "Is that your only skill? Why don't you call me your darling, your angel, your sweetheart, your kitten, your rosebud and dearest delight? It was soon over, that great love of yours!"

Very softly, the thief essayed a new version of his litany. "May the Almighty look with favour on this house," he mouthed. "I was sent here by Your Excellency's cousin and godson, Herr von Tornefeld, who's detained at the mill . . ."

"I promised you a cavalryman's love," said the man in the bed, "but a cavalryman's love is short-lived. It's no more enduring than grass in a meadow or dew on a field."

"So I'm not your sweetheart and kitten and rosebud and dearest delight?"

"You're as greedy for pretty speeches as a child for gruel and honey. Didn't I present you with a silk ribbon seven ells long, and two twists of sugar, and a silver thaler with St George on it?"

"Yes, but you wearied of our sport too soon. Your oil is all used up and your little lamp has gone out. It didn't burn for long."

"Herr von Tornefeld – Your Excellency knows him –" muttered the thief, "he's detained at the mill and requests an alamode coat and a braided hat and money and a carriage and horses . . ."

"That comes of fasting," said the man in the bed. "I keep all fast days. I go in quest of salvation like a huntsman after wild boar – it makes a man forgetful of the pleasures of the flesh. When I'm rich I'll employ a chaplain to pray and fast in my place."

"Better employ a chaplain man enough to take your place when you bed a virgin."

"That's enough!" the man exclaimed with sudden vehemence. "You claim to have been a virgin? You think I failed to perceive you weren't intact? Your flower wasn't worth the plucking."

"But that's not all," the thief muttered, still intent on Herr von Tornefeld. "He also wants a dressing-gown, Your Excellency, and some stockings and neckerchiefs and two wigs . . ."

"What a boorish thing to say!" cried the girl in the bed. "Virgin or not, you yourself aren't intact. You've only one ear and one eye."

"I got those wounds from my enemies," the man said proudly, still incensed.

34

"And I got mine from my friends," the girl retorted with a chuckle. At that the man bellowed with laughter, and for a while they remained unaware that a third person had joined in their merriment, for the thief found all this pillow-talk hilarious in the extreme.

"Hush!" the girl said suddenly. "What was that? There's someone in the room."

"You fool!" said the man. "Who would be here in the room? How could he have got in?"

"There's someone in the room, I tell you — I heard him laugh," the girl insisted. She sat up and peered into the gloom, and the faint glow from the stove fell on her white bosom.

"Lie down and leave me in peace," the man told her. "I posted a dragoon outside the door — he wouldn't have admitted anyone. With your ears, you'd hear fish singing in the sea."

"There! There he is!" the girl cried in a piercing voice. She gripped her bedmate by the arm and pointed into the darkness. "There he is, over against the wall! Help, Help!"

The man tore himself free and leapt out of bed. His sword was in his hand in a trice.

"Hey, you there!" he called. "Who are you? What are you doing here? Stand still or I'll slice you up and have you carried out piecemeal. Stay where you are or I'll run you through the belly!"

The thief, seeing that things had taken an unforeseen turn, thought it high time to quit the shadows and tell his lordship who had sent him and on what business.

"God bless you, sir," he said hurriedly, with a low but invisible bow. "Your Excellency's godson sent me, so here I am at Your Excellency's service. He's waiting at the mill —"

"Balthazar!" called the man with the sword. "Come in here and strike a light! I wish to see this fellow who prates of God and godsons."

"No light, no light!" the girl screeched. "I'm as naked as Eve."

"Then back into Paradise with you!" said the man, thrusting her down in bed and tossing a blanket over her head. Meantime, the dragoon had hurried in and lit the wax candles on the table. The thief found himself confronted by a short, thickset man brandishing a sword, naked save for a shirt and a feathered hat.

The thief was transfixed with terror. He recognised the man as the captain of dragoons known far and wide as "the Bloody Baron", who was evidently quartered here.

The Bloody Baron was so called because he had undertaken to butcher the bands of robbers that ravaged Silesia and Bohemia. Invested with judicial authority by the emperor himself, he prowled the countryside unceasingly at the head of his dragoons, and all who preyed on other people's property – vagrants and pickpockets, highwaymen and thieves, miscreants great and small – feared him like Satan personified. The hangman who accompanied him never had rope enough. To him, a lenient sentence meant branding on the forehead followed by a lifetime of servitude in the Venetian galleys. It was to escape death at the hands of this man and his dragoons that the thief had thought to take refuge in the bishop's inferno, and now ill luck had brought him to this room. The Bloody Baron stood facing him a mere five paces away, and the house was swarming with dragoons. There was no way out, no hope of giving his captors the slip. The thief's numb terror was mingled with a trace of surprise that the dreaded Bloody Baron should be so small of stature and his chest and legs so apelike in their hairiness.

Having covered his blind eye with a square of black cloth suspended from a ribbon – the start of his toilette – the captain took his leather riding breeches and belt from the dragoon.

"Now to discover who you are, fellow," he said, "but have a care! Do you see this sword of mine?"

The thief realised that bravado alone could save him now. If he showed fear he was done for.

"Yes, I see your sword, what of it?" he retorted. "There's room on it for three dozen sparrows. You could slice off seven heads of cabbage at a stroke."

36

"He has a loose tongue and eyes like a vicious horse," said the dragoon, who had knelt to pull on his captain's boots. "If he knew whom he was addressing, he'd sing a different song."

"Your neck's at stake, fellow," growled the captain. "Any more of that, and I'll have you taken outside and beaten till your own brother wouldn't know you."

"Leave me be," the thief protested. "My business isn't with you. It wasn't you I sought."

"How dare you take that tone to a nobleman and an officer!" the captain roared. "I can see I shall have to teach you some respect and good manners, so that you can properly introduce yourself to the Devil in Hell when I hang you. What were you doing in my bedchamber? Answer me!"

"What was I doing?" the thief replied in a peevish, impatient voice, as if he had no time to waste on the questioner or his questions. "I was looking for the owner of this house, of course."

"You were, were you?" The captain turned to the bed. "Is he from hereabouts, Margret? Do you know him?"

More dragoons had entered in the meantime, and the acrid smoke of their torches filled the room. The girl who had spotted the thief in the darkness was now sitting on the edge of the bed. Unseen by the dragoons, she had hurriedly pulled her chemise over her head and clamped her skirt between her knees. It was a moment or two before she answered.

"No, he's not from hereabouts. I never saw him before."

The captain strode over to the thief, boots squeaking.

"Lousy, scabby, filthy, and in rags," he said with a laugh. "He doesn't look as if my lord bishop sent him here with an invitation to dinner. Search the man! He's a member of Black Ibitz's band, I'll be bound."

Two dragoons seized the thief and felt in his pockets. One of them found the knife he always carried and held it aloft.

"I told you so," said the captain. "He meant to do away with me. Well, fellow, speak: what was that knife doing in your pocket?"

The thief gave a despairing laugh. "It's a rare piece brought

37

me by the Spanish Fleet," he blurted out, his throat tight with fear. "I sent for it from the New World, to cut my bread and cheese."

"You'll not be cutting much more bread and cheese," said the captain. He addressed the room at large. "He stole into my bedroom, meaning to wait until I was asleep and then dispatch me with that knife. Lienhard, come here. Ibitz and his men held you prisoner for three days. See if he's one of them."

The dragoon held his torch close to the thief's face.

"No, he's not one of Ibitz's men," he said. "I know them all – Afrom, Crooked Michel, Owlface, Gallowsmeat, Whistling Boy, and the Brabanter – but not this fellow. Besides, Your Excellency, we have them all surrounded. None of them can escape."

"One lone man would not find it so hard to slip past our sentries," said the captain. "After all, he stole into the house unobserved. The Devil may trust him, not I."

"But he's not one of Ibitz's men," the dragoon said firmly. "There are twenty of them. Tinsmith Hannes, Sainted Jonas, Klaproth, Veiland, Feuerbaum and Mad Matthes – I know them all, but not him."

"So tell me who sent you!" the captain bellowed at the thief. "Speak or I'll have you bent and stretched, so help me God!"

"I was sent by the nobleman whose servant I am, Your Excellency, and that's the honest truth." The thief, mindful that he had Tornefeld's signet ring as proof of his good faith, was gradually regaining his courage. "I have a message for the owner of this demesne."

"Who is your master?" the captain broke in. "By God, the nobility hereabouts employ strange lackeys. What nobleman is it that keeps such a ragged fellow in his service?"

"My master is his lordship's youthful cousin and godson," said the thief. "His lordship stood sponsor at his christening, and –"

The captain roared with laughter.

"His lordship's godson sent you?" he exclaimed. "The devil

38

you say! In that case, welcome to this house. Since you come from his lordship's godson, may your mission be crowned with success. How old is this famous youngster of a godson, pray?"

"Eighteen or twenty, at a guess – I haven't known him long," said the thief, puzzled by the Bloody Baron's laughter and singular manner.

The girl, who was now fully dressed, threaded her way through the dragoons and stepped up to the thief.

"Lies cannot save you, poor man," she said. "The owner of this house has no godson. No more lies, poor man. You would do better to go down on your knees and beg for Christian mercy."

"No, by all that's holy, no!" cried the captain. "I want to see him sweat like a chicken on the spit, so on with the game! He wishes me to conduct him to the owner of this manor. Very well, his wish shall be granted. Fellow, come with me. Balthazar, my gloves and scarf!"

With his hands bound behind his back, the thief followed the captain upstairs escorted by two dragoons carrying candles. Now that he was to see Herr von Krechwitz at last, curiosity pricked him more than ever. A new mystery had reared its head: Why should the Bloody Baron, the mortal foe and arch-persecutor whom he mentally consigned to perdition, have burst out laughing when told that he, the thief, had been sent by the godson of the owner of the house? And the girl who had shared the captain's bed – why had she denied the existence of such a godson? What manner of man was it that had no godson at all, when even the poorest day-labourer had one? Was Herr von Krechwitz such a dissolute monster that no mother wished him to stand sponsor at her child's baptism? Was this lord of the manor a Turk, a Tatar, or a Moor? Or was he such a miser that he begrudged a baby its baptismal thaler? Or was he . . .

For a moment, sheer surprise stopped the thief in his tracks. The truth had dawned on him at last. Had his hands not been bound behind his back, he would have smitten his brow. All was clear to him now. He now understood why everyone on this estate was dishonest – why the workfolk were unruly and the fields neglected, why the sheep-shed harboured splenic fever – and he cursed himself for a fool and a blockhead because he'd taken so long to divine the reason. "A poor ewe-lamb to be fleeced by all and sundry," he told himself with a grim smile, clenching his fists. The captain had paused outside the half-open door of the "Long Room". He knocked, then strode in with a nobleman's ceremonious self-assurance, and the dragoons thrust the thief into the room in his wake.

Yes, it was as just he had surmised: the owner of Kleinroop Manor was a mere child, a girl of seventeen at most, and as slim and dainty as an angel. There were tears in her eyes, the thief could see that at once, and facing her with his elbow propped on the chimney-piece was Baron von Saltza auf Düsterloh und Pencke, the fork-bearded nobleman and usurer to whom the bailiff had sold his young mistress's greyhound and saddle-horse.

The captain planted himself in front of her, plumed hat in hand, and bowed.

"Do I come at an inopportune moment?" he began. "I trust that your ladyship will pardon me for intruding at this late hour, but I must saddle up at crack of dawn and would have deemed it shameful to depart without paying my respects, the more so because I hope to preserve a humble place in your ladyship's thoughts."

The girl smiled and inclined her head.

"You do me too much honour, captain," she said in a soft, gentle voice. "It saddens me to hear that you mean to leave so soon. Were you not satisfied with your quarters?"

The thief gazed at her intently. All his plans lay in ruins.

"It's a pity," he said to himself. "She's so young, she'll never believe me if I tell her that her workfolk are a bunch of scheming rogues. Being a child, she still thinks the world an honest place. She'll never believe me if I cite chapter and verse to prove that she and her people could live on the milk and poultry alone and sell the surplus at market. Her bailiff will have told her otherwise, so every word would be a waste of breath. She's beautiful, though. I've never seen anything lovelier in my life . . ."

"My quarters are most comfortable, I could wish for no better," the captain assured her with a bow. "All was perfectly à point, but I'm off to settle accounts with Black Ibitz and his band of villains. We have them surrounded in the Fox's Earth, and I must join my men by daybreak tomorrow, when the hunt commences."

"That's life for you," muttered the thief, who was standing in the doorway between the two dragoons. "He'll harry those robbers in their lair with axe and rope, and they're only poor folk, but he neither sees nor molests the robbers here in this house, who brazenly waste their mistress's substance . . ."

"May your mission be crowned with success, Captain," said the girl. "Ibitz and his band have wrought havoc, both hereabouts and in Poland. One hears talk every day of their attacking some waggoner or driving off some farmer's cattle. Truly, Captain, you're a second St George."

"But they're only poor folk," muttered the thief, while the Bloody Baron, gratified by this tribute, stroked his luxuriant moustache. "Had they been granted a daily morsel of bread and a thatched roof over their heads, they would have remained honest, but that's the way of the world. Meantime, the rabble here on this estate . . ."

"I beg your ladyship's leave to depart," Fork-Beard interposed in a harsh voice. "I must see to it that I reach home in good time. If your ladyship should change her mind, I shall be as ready to oblige and accommodate her tomorrow as I am today."

"If only my noble godfather would allow me to keep Jason and Diana . . ." said the girl, and her eyes filled anew with tears.

"Your ladyship can have as many saddle-horses as she pleases," said Fork-Beard. "The matter rests with her alone.

Fine clothes, necklaces, rings, guests every day, a respected place in society – all these are hers for the asking."

"It distresses me that I cannot do as my noble godfather wishes," said the girl, and her voice hardened. "You know it cannot be, any more than the sun can stray from its course. I have pledged my heart and hand to another, and I shall wait for him, if need be, till Judgement Day."

"May your ladyship never regret that decision," Fork-Beard said brusquely. "Meantime, I remain at your service. Are the horses harnessed up?"

"Heaven preserve the young lady!" the thief said in a horrified whisper. "Can he really have designs on her, the depraved old brute? They're as ill-matched as lampblack and virgin snow . . ."

"The horses are harnessed up," the girl replied. "The sleigh and driver await you in the courtyard." She paused. "I had pinned my hopes on your generosity, godfather. If you would only let me keep Jason . . ."

"Out of the question," Fork Beard snarled. "I bought that mare and that hound myself – I paid good money for them. If economies had been practised in this house, things would never have come to such a pass. One kreuzer begets another, one guilder spawns two, but no one here seems to know that. When firewood won't burn, your kitchen-maid kindles it with butter by the pound."

"What need have you of a thoroughbred hound?" the captain called from the door. "For hunting, a farm-bred mongrel would serve you quite as well."

Fork-Beard turned and looked him haughtily up and down.

"Oblige me, sir, by attending to your own business," he snarled. "I've never meddled in yours. My enemies hereabouts are legion, I know, but many a man would gladly take my place."

The captain drew himself up with a grimace of contempt.

"I'm a poor man," he said. "All I possess is my imperial warrant and my good name, but I wouldn't step into your shoes for a thousand thalers."

42

"Look to your own shoes, not mine – they're not for sale!" bellowed Fork-Beard, pop-eyed and puce with anger. "Out of my way, sir, I'm going!"

"What was that you said?" the captain inquired calmly. "Beware of apoplexy, sir. You shouldn't puff yourself up so – you'll burst like Judas on the gallows."

"Like Judas on the gallows?" cried Fork-Beard, gasping for breath. "You forget whom you're addressing, sir. I too am of noble birth. Have a care: I wear a sword, and it sits loosely in the scabbard."

The captain stepped aside and gestured toward the open door.

"Entirely at your service, sir. I shall gladly do you the courtesy of crossing swords with you in the courtyard, nobleman to nobleman."

"Just as you please, sir, just as you please," said Fork-Beard, who had now reached the door, "but I don't have time to listen to you further. Another time – I have pressing business elsewhere."

And he set off down the stairs as fast as dignity permitted. The captain stared after him for a moment, then turned to the girl.

"I beg your ladyship's pardon for saying so," he said, flourishing his hat, "but that godfather of yours is, with all due respect and devotion, a blackguard. A sword-thrust would be too good for him. I'd rather pay a street urchin to punch him on the nose."

"He keeps pressing me to marry him," the girl said with a weary smile. "He has offered to relieve me of all my burdens out of friendship for my late lamented father."

"If that's friendship," exclaimed the captain, "I'd sooner seek it among the wolves of the forest. Your ladyship is betrothed, I gather. May I be permitted to inquire the name of the man fortunate enough to be able to boast of your ladyship's affection?"

The thief awoke from a kind of dream. He had caught himself yielding to a strange delusion: that he was no longer a

43

thief but the man to whom this high-born damsel had pledged herself – that he was holding her in his arms with her cheek against his own.

He gave a start. "No, no," he whispered with a deep but inaudible sigh, "may God in his mercy turn my heart from what can never be mine . . ."

"You've always been good to me, Captain, so I'll tell you," the girl was saying. "My betrothed is a Swedish nobleman, a friend from my earliest childhood. He has my ring and I have his, but it's long since I had news of him. 'He has forgotten you,' I often think, 'but you'll never forget him.' At other times my hopes revive and I feel that happiness is speeding toward me post-haste. His name is Christian. He's a godson of my late father's and a cousin on my mother's side."

"Can he really be the one?" the thief wondered in boundless amazement. "I'd never have thought it possible. So her heart belongs to that callow youth, that weakling who can't talk big enough when he's toasting his toes at the fire but whimpers and wails without cease when the frost nips his ears. She's keeping faith with a mouse of a nobleman who never gives her a thought. His heart is set on the war and Charles of Sweden, but only if he has a fur bonnet to keep out the cold, and an alamode coat, and a carriage and horses, and pockets full of money, and silk stockings, and taffeta and satin enough to wipe his nose on, and God alone knows what else . . ."

"*What* did your ladyship say?" asked the captain. "A godson to your ladyship's late lamented father? This fellow I've brought with me – can it be that he was telling the truth after all? Come here, you quintessence of all gallow's-birds! Pay your respects to her ladyship and say who sent you."

The thief stepped forward and bowed, but he shunned the light cast by the oil-lamp's two bright little flames and kept his face in shadow. "I must say nothing," it flashed through his mind, "nothing – not a word about that boy!" As to why he felt so constrained to remain silent and disguise the fact that Tornefeld had sent him, even he had yet to discover the reason.

44

"Why stand there hanging your head?" the captain told him angrily. "Speak! Say who sent you!"

"No, no no!" cried a voice inside him. "She mustn't know. If she does, she'll go and sell all she has left. The clothes in her closet, the lace at her neck, her bed linen – she'll sell them all to provide that boy with fancy coats and silk stockings. She mustn't learn the truth!"

He avoided her gaze and said quietly, "No one sent me."

"So now it's 'No one sent me'," the captain exclaimed. "Earlier you spoke of a nobleman and told me you were sent by him."

The thief drew a deep breath. "I lied," he said.

"I thought as much," growled the captain. "He was trying to talk his way out of the noose."

The girl walked over to the thief with noiseless, gliding tread and paused in front of him, but he turned his face away rather than look her in the eye.

"Where do you hail from, you poor man?" she asked. "You've come far, from the look of you – your face is pinched with hunger. Quickly, go down to the kitchen and have the maid crumble you some bread in a bowl of soup. First, though, tell me if Christian Tornefeld sent you to me. Where is he, and why did he not come himself?"

"If I tell her," the thief reflected, "she'll go to him. If she doesn't have a carriage and horses, she'll brave the snow on foot." And he seemed to see Tornefeld's smiling face. The boy was holding her in his arms just as he himself had held her for a moment in his wild imaginings.

He stared at the floor. "I'm unacquainted with the gentleman," he replied. "I know nothing of him."

"I thought as much!" the captain said again. "How would this wretched tinker be acquainted with a gentleman of quality? He's one of Ibitz's gang, or I'm a Dutchman." He turned on the thief. "Now, fellow, tell us what or whom you were after when you stole into this house."

The thief felt the cold sweat break out on his brow. His last hour seemed nigh, but he clung to his decision: for good or ill, he would never let the captain wrest the truth from him.

"I came to steal," he said in a defiant tone.

"In that case," said the captain, "the gibbet shall have its due. Make your peace with God, fellow. You must hang."

The girl gave a low cry. "No, don't hang him! He looks so poor and wretched, I'll warrant he's never known a single day's happiness in his life."

"He looks so godless and infamous, I'd credit him with any piece of mischief," the captain said, scowling. "I know better than your ladyship how to deal with the likes of him."

"Don't hang him," the girl entreated, raising her hands. "He did nothing. His only crime is to be poor and half-starved. Let him go, Captain – let him go for my sake."

The thief stood there transfixed. Never before had he heard anyone utter such words. Folk had cursed and beaten him all his life, threatened him with gaol and the gallows. Children had pelted him with stones in the street, yet this high-born damsel had taken pity on him. Having looked death defiantly in the face, he now had the strangest sensation. His throat tightened and his cheeks twitched convulsively. He would have given anything to do the girl a service of some kind, but he still didn't tell her – couldn't tell her – that Tornefeld was waiting at the mill.

"Your ladyship knows that my dearest wish is to serve her – she has only to command," the captain said with ill-concealed annoyance. "The fellow's a bad lot, but since your ladyship insists . . . Sirrah, you owe your escape from the gallows to her ladyship's gracious intercession."

The lingering howl of a dog drifted up from the courtyard.

"I'm much obliged to you, Captain, and I'll not forget it," the girl said quickly. "That was Jason, did you hear? He's pining for my company – I believe he can sense that he and Diana are about to be taken from me. I must go and bid my dear old friends farewell."

She hurried from the room and down the stairs. The captain walked slowly after her. At the door he turned.

"I'll be damned if he isn't one of Ibitz's band," he told the dragoons. "He may have escaped a hanging, but not a thrashing. Take him and tan his hide – give him five-and-twenty of the best, then let him go. He can run and tell his master, Black Ibitz, that I'll come for him tomorrow with fire and steel. There'll be a fine day's hunting in the Fox's Earth."

The thief stood below in the courtyard, his face to the wall, while two dragoons held him by the arms and a third wielded the hazel switch. Blow after blow came whistling down on his bare back. Meantime, not a hundred paces distant, the youthful lady of the manor was taking leave of her dearest companions. The dog jumped up at her, barking, as she clasped her mare around the neck. "Farewell, Diana," she said in a voice brimming with sorrow and affection. "I've always held you dear. And you, my Jason, God protect you, for we must go our separate ways." Fork-Beard, a thickly muffled figure ensconced in the sleigh, smote his fists together impatiently. Her adieus were taking too long for his taste.

The thief did not witness this valedictory scene, he only heard the dog barking and the horse whinnying. The hazel switch continued to whistle through the air, but he never flinched. "Lay on, lay on!" he hissed through his clenched teeth. "I'm not of noble blood, perhaps, but I'm not a common usurer. Lay on, lay on! I'm only of humble birth, but I don't make money and horses and carriages out of other folks' poverty. Lay on, lay on! What a noble crew they are, Fork-Beard, who ran from the captain's sword, and Tornefeld, the would-be warrior who fears to get his fingers frozen! Lay on, lay on! I'm of different mettle – I'd make a better nobleman than either of them."

And an outrageous thought took shape in his feverish brain: he fancied that he was indeed a nobleman, not a vagrant and thief, and that he must return and instil order into the estate and its workfolk, for everything here – the girl, the manor, the farm buildings and fields – was destined to be his. "I've sat long enough at the table of the poor," he grunted. "Now I've a mind to sit at the master's table." Born in the throes of

47

searing pain, this thought possessed him, and every stroke that came whistling down on his back burned it deeper into his soul.

Not that he noticed, his chastisement had ended. The hazel switch was tossed aside and landed in the snow. One of the dragoons returned the thief's shirt and jacket and gave him a swig of brandy from his canteen.

"Now be off with you," he urged, "before our captain sets eyes on you again."

They took him under the arms and began to lead him toward the gate, thinking that his legs might give way, but he spurned their assistance and walked off through the snow, unsteady but erect. In the gateway he turned. He could see the girl and the house and the courtyard and the overturned harrow jutting from the snow, and his gaze embraced them all as if they were already his. Then he strode on. The wind lashed his face, the snow crunched beneath his feet, and the maple trees flanking the drive bowed their wind-whipped branches to the ground as if prescient of the future: as if, in bowing to the man who was leaving the manor behind him, they were saluting its future lord and master.

He had as yet no plan in mind when he passed through Lancken village with its yapping dogs and wailing bagpipe and took the road that led to the mill. He knew only that his back was smarting, and that he must return as a nobleman on horseback with plumes in his hat and money in every pocket. He couldn't, after all, keep his promise to the miller and enter the bishop's inferno. "I haven't yet resigned myself to hell," he muttered as he trudged through the knee-deep snow. "Did we strike a bargain? No! No bargain is well and truly struck until it's sealed with a glass of brandy. The miller begrudged me a brandy, so now he has only himself to blame. The dragoon that held me while the other flogged me – *he* gave me brandy to drink afterwards. Yes, brother! Thanks, brother! I drank to my return. *That* bargain stands. Yes, brother, *that* bargain was well and truly struck."

48

Into the bishop's hell on earth? Never! That was a thing of the past. He would return to the world and join battle once more with the powers that had opposed him throughout his life. Tempted by the great game of chance, he would hazard one more throw of the dice. To him, who had never once contrived to trick frugal countryfolk out of food enough to eat his fill, it now seemed that all the world's gold was his for the taking.

He needed and must somehow acquire the arcanum of which Tornefeld had made so much. That piece of sacred parchment, or whatever else it might be, was the key to all wealth and happiness. Let Tornefeld see how well he fared without it in the Swedish army.

In the Swedish army? No, Tornefeld must never join the Swedish army, never return on horseback in plumed hat and handsome clothes. *She* loved him – he was dear to *her* heart, so he would have to vanish for ever. "Into the bishop's inferno with him!" muttered the thief, and at that moment it occurred to him how he could rid himself of Tornefeld and keep his promise to the miller's ghost: Tornefeld would enter the bishop's inferno in his place. For nine years? For all eternity! Once under the lash of the overseer and his foremen, that mother's boy of a nobleman would not last two months. Stronger men than he had succumbed before their nine years were up.

And then, while these thoughts were passing through the thief's mind, he seemed to see Tornefeld lying in the snow at his feet, as he had that very morning, devoid of hope and mortally tired, and he was once more overcome with pity for the youngster who had lain there babbling about his nobleman's honour. "On your feet, friend!" he wanted to say – "On your feet, I won't abandon you!" But he stifled his compassion. It couldn't be: Tornefeld must disappear for ever. "Farewell, farewell!" he shouted into the teeth of the snow-laden gale. "There's nothing more I can do for you. The girl I saw weeping – I cannot banish her from my heart." So saying, he took leave of his comrade in adversity. So saying, he passed sentence on Christian Tornefeld.

49

When the thief was a stone's throw from the mill, its ghostly owner, still clad in his waggoner's smock and feathered hat, loomed up ahead of him as suddenly as if he had sprung from the ground. The thief would have slipped past, but there were deep snow-drifts to left and right, and the miller refused to budge.

"Let me pass," said the thief, his teeth chattering. "I wish to go inside. It's cold, and the night will turn still colder. I heard the cry of the screech-owl."

"Why should you care if the night turns colder?" the miller demanded with a chuckle as hollow as if it had issued from the depths of a well. "You'll not freeze. You'll learn this very night how to rake coals from a fiery furnace."

"Not tonight," said the thief, who had plucked up courage again. "Grant me until tomorrow. Today is Wednesday – an unlucky day, for that was when Our Lord Jesus was betrayed."

He had thought that the ghost would promptly vanish and return to Purgatory at the sound of Christ's holy name, but the miller continued to stand there looking him in the face.

"I cannot wait," he said, shaking the snow from his smock. "You must come with me tonight. Tomorrow I'll be gone."

"I know, I know," groaned the thief, and a shiver ran down his spine. "Tomorrow you'll be a little heap of dust and ashes. Let me go, sir. I'll say a *Miserere* for you and a *De profundis* – those are the favourite fare of poor dead souls."

"What are you blathering about, you numskull?" the miller exclaimed. "You can keep your *De profundis*. Tomorrow at cock-crow I leave for Venice to fetch merchandise for my noble master: crystal goblets, bolts of velvet, gilded wall-paper, and two of the new Spanish lap-dogs."

"What need has your bishop of gilded wall-paper and bolts of velvet?" growled the thief, who had always disliked the high and the mighty. "He should share his wealth with the poor of the land, not live in luxury and splendour."

"My gracious lord is a secular prince as well as a bishop," the miller explained. "The man you see riding in a gilded carriage and six – that's the prince. But go to Mass on Lady

Day and you'll see the bishop, a devout, modest, and altogether holy man."

"What if the Devil carries off the secular prince?" the thief said sarcastically. "What becomes of the bishop then?"

"Silence!" cried the miller, filled with indignation. "What an uncouth tongue you have, fellow! Now come with me and learn to earn your bread by honest toil."

But the thief remained where he was.

"Circumstances have changed," he said. "I shall not be going with you after all."

"Did I hear aright?" the miller exclaimed. "You've lost your taste for an easy life? You fool! War and slaughter, fire and pestilence are raging on every side, but the bishop's domain is at peace."

"Peace is not the thing I seek," the thief replied. "I wish to go out into the world and prove myself as a free man."

"It's too late for that," the miller said angrily. "We struck a bargain, so you must come with me. I hold you to your word."

"You cannot hold me to my word," the thief retorted. "No bargain is properly struck until it has been sealed with a glass of brandy. I've no notion how it is in hell, but that's the custom here on earth."

"Brandy be damned!" cried the miller. "I plied you generously with bread and sausage and beer."

"You'll be paid your due," the thief told him. "My companion who sits in your parlour over yonder – he'll go with you in my place."

"That fellow?" the miller said indignantly. "It's you I want. Why should I take that idle youth? He's no use to me – he eats more than he's worth. He'll cost my noble master more in a day than he'll earn him in a week."

"He's weakened by hunger and hardship," said the thief. "Let him but regain his strength, and you'll see how well he can wield a crowbar and break rock from a quarry barehanded."

"You're the one I want!" the miller bellowed. He came close

to the thief and caught him by the jacket. "It was you I struck the bargain with. I'll not let you go."

The thief felt the nightmarish weight of the miller's icy hand on his chest. He fought for breath, and his heart seemed constricted by bands of iron. It was clear to him that this poor soul from Purgatory was endowed with superhuman strength. He strove to escape, but in vain. And then, in his extremity, he remembered the spell – the form of words that would exorcise a ghost – and recited it in a quavering, breathless voice:

In Jesu's name and Mary's,
go down upon your knees,
and pray that Child and Virgin
your soul from sin release.

"What's that you're bawling?" the miller demanded. "This is no time for prayer!" But he was down on his knees, and the thief found that he could breathe and move once more: the nightmarish weight had gone from his chest. "Help me up!" cried the miller. "Why the devil did you push me? See, now I'm kneeling in the snow."

The thief was convinced that he hadn't pushed the miller at all. The formula that had sprung to his lips in the nick of time – that was what had compelled the ghost to release him and fall on its knees.

"Have I your leave to go?" he asked, bending down.

"Go where you please, no one needs you," snapped the miller. He seized the thief's hand and hauled himself erect. "That gibberish of yours was enough to show me what manner of man you are. Hurry off to the gibbet and find someone to hang you. I want no more to do with you."

The way to the mill was now open. The thief walked on, chuckling to himself. He had won the battle. He was no longer in thrall to the ghost of the man who left his grave for one day each year in quest of living flesh and blood with which to repay a pfennig of his debt to his former master, the bishop. He did, however, have another battle to win: a battle with Tornefeld, who must disappear into the bishop's inferno, leaving him, the thief, in possession of his noble name and the arcanum that guaranteed good fortune.

Tornefeld jumped up from the bench beside the stove as soon as the thief walked in.

"At last!" he said petulantly, rubbing his eyes. "You've kept an honest cavalier waiting long enough, in all conscience!"

The thief made haste to shut the door behind him, for the wind had blown a cloud of wet snowflakes into the room.

"I came as fast as I could," he said. "What's more, I had good reason."

"Well?" Tornefeld demanded. "What news of my affairs?"

"Bad news," said the thief, hanging up his patched and threadbare coat to dry in front of the stove. "It will scarcely gladden your heart."

"Didn't you speak with my noble godfather?" asked Tornefeld.

"No," the thief replied. "He's gone by special mail to the world hereafter. He grants no audiences these days."

"Is that the truth?" Tornefeld cried. "Is he really dead?"

"I swear it," said the thief. "As sure as I hope for salvation, he's dead. But friend, how downcast and forlorn you look!"

"Dead," Tornefeld murmured in dismay. "My noble god-father dead, and I'd pinned all my hopes on him. He was my father's cousin and good friend, God rest them both. Who presides over the estate now?"

"A girl," said the thief, gazing into the fire. "A mere child. So kind, so young – as beautiful as a seraph come to earth."

"The demoiselle his daughter, Maria Agneta, *ma cousine!*" Tornefeld exclaimed. "If she's still there, I'm saved. Did you speak with her?"

"Yes," the thief lied, "but she couldn't call you to mind at first. Only when I showed her the ring –"

"Ah," Tornefeld broke in delightedly, "*then* she knew who had sent you! Did you tell her that I'm here at the mill, and that I need a carriage and horses and a coat and –"

The thief persisted in his lie.

"Yes, but she refused me. She's poor. She herself can barely make ends meet, she told me. The estate is in debt. No money in the house, horses and carriages in pledge. 'My cousin must make his own way to the Swedish army,' she said."

"No money?" Tornefeld repeated sadly. "Ah, but you should have seen Kleinroop Manor in the old days: never a day without fire beneath the spit, or guests at table, or fish in the trough, or game in the larder. As for money, my noble godfather could have built three churches with twelve spires, he was so wealthy."

He fell silent and hung his head.

"So the demoiselle didn't remember me?" he continued with a weary smile. "Years have gone by since I saw her last, it's true. We were children, the two of us. We swore eternal love and devotion, but that's forgotten – buried beneath the sands of time."

He paced the room before coming to a halt beside the thief.

"I'm alone in the world – alone and without a patron – but I must join the Swedish army notwithstanding. I must!"

"You aspire to fly like a falcon and have no feathers," the thief said scornfully. "Your king will manage very well without you."

"Enough!" cried Tornefeld. "Do you take me for a rogue because my pockets are empty? I'm a Swede and a nobleman, and I must go to my king. I shall leave this very night."

He slapped his thigh as if his sword still hung there, then went to the window.

"There's a driving, whistling, snow-laden wind," he said uneasily. "It's a night to rival the jaws of hell."

"Yes," said the thief, "even the wolves are confessing their sins tonight, yet you're for the road. You'll not get far, my friend – no farther than your tombstone."

"I shall travel by day in short stages," said Tornefeld, "and sleep beside farmhouse stoves at night. A bowl of gruel and a mug of beer – the peasants will give me that much for charity's sake. I shall leave tomorrow at daybreak."

"Alas, my friend," the thief said with simulated regret, "you've yet to hear the worst. Those musketeers! I'd give anything to help you, but I fear you're already on the threshold of eternity."

"The threshold of eternity? What musketeers? What are you saying?" Tornefeld's voice had begun to shake and his forehead was beaded with sweat. "I implore you by the living God to tell me all you know."

"The imperial musketeers have condemned you, as a deserter, to forfeit life, limb, and honour."

"I know that," said Tornefeld, passing a hand across his brow, "but they're far away."

"No, my friend, they're not," lied the thief. "The imperial musketeers are billeted on the estate a company strong, and their captain . . . Jesus Christ!"

He stared at the bench beside the stove. On it, not that either man had seen him enter, sat the miller in his red jerkin. He lolled there with his legs crossed, teeth bared and lips set in a crooked smile. Just then he began to sing in a discordant voice:

> Who rides at a trot
> 'twixt saucepan and pot
> yet stirs not an inch from the spot?
> Who dances a measure
> at Lucifer's pleasure –

"Enough of that, I've no wish to hear it!" Tornefeld shouted at the miller, his face convulsed. He turned again to the thief.

"Is that the truth? You actually encountered the musketeers?"

Tornefeld was beside himself with fear, the thief could clearly see, but he felt not a scrap of pity for him. His heart had turned to stone.

"May I be hewn in pieces if what I say isn't true," he declared with a nervous, sidelong glance at the miller's ghost. "I came as fast as I could to warn you. When the captain heard you were at the mill, he swore in my presence to see you hanged, and his corporals sat around the fire throwing dice for the privilege of marching you to the gallows."

Tornefeld cried out as if the noose were already about his neck, and drops of sweat trickled down his cheeks.

"I must go," he gasped. "They mustn't find me here. Don't abandon me, friend. Help me to escape – I'll be grateful to you for the rest of my days."

The thief shrugged his shoulders helplessly.

"The snow lies deep," he said. "You'll never outrun them. They'll overtake you in the end."

He was still speaking when the miller broke into song once more, croaking the words like a raven and beating time with his hands:

> Who dances a measure
> at Lucifer's pleasure?
> Who prances around
> to the sinister sound
> of Death playing the final gavotte?

"Silence, sir, unless you mean to provoke me," cried Tornefeld. "I won't tolerate it, d'you hear?" Furiously, he reached for the hilt of his missing sword, but an instant later he was once more overcome with mortal fear. He called the thief his blood brother and dearest friend and implored him, with upraised hands, to help him cheat the gallows for God and His Passion's sake.

The thief pretended to deliberate.

"Being as sorry for you as I am," he said, "I've a mind to help you for the sake of brotherly love. You meant to join the Swedish army, but a nobleman on the road encounters many traps and pitfalls which a common man can more easily evade. Give me the arcanum you carry hidden beneath your coat and I'll go to the Swedish army in your place."

"The arcanum?" Tornefeld exclaimed. "Never! I promised my father on his death-bed that I would deliver it into the king's own hands."

"Do as I say or you'll hang," the thief said coolly. "A man can die for his king as well on the gallows as in the field. The musketeers will be here within the hour. You know yourself what the consequence will be."

Tornefeld buried his face in his hands and groaned.

"Friend," he said softly, "I'll tell you the truth: my courage leaves much to be desired. I want to save my life – I'm devilish afraid of death and eternity. Here, take it."

He reached inside his coat and produced the arcanum, which proved to be a printed book. The thief took it from him with both hands and held it tight for fear he might take it back.

"That bible belonged to Gustavus Adolphus – he had it beneath his corselet when he fell at Lützen," said Tornefeld. "Its pages are stained with his royal blood. My father was given it by his father, who commanded the Blues in that battle. You must put it into the king's own hands. I had hoped that it would bring me honour and advancement in the Swedish army. Perhaps it will be the making of your own good fortune." He paused. "But what, friend, is to become of me?"

The thief had already stowed the bible away beneath his coat.

"Where I shall take you, no more harm can come to you," he said. "I was promised employment in the bishop's stamp-mill. By taking my place you'll be safe from the musketeers, for the bishop exercises his own jurisdiction. You'll remain in the bishop's employ, serving him honestly, until the regiment's case against you has been set aside and annulled."

"Serving him honestly – yes, indeed I will," said Tornefeld, "and may God reward you here below and in heaven above."

"Is the bargain struck?" called the miller from his place beside the stove. "If so, you shall seal it with a glass or two of Strasbourg brandy wine."

He rose and placed a bottle and two glasses on the table, but Tornefeld shook his head.

"I'm not in a festive mood," he said in a subdued voice. "Ah, friend, how low I've fallen!"

"Better low than aloft on the scaffold," the thief told him.

"Life is a precious but fragile possession. The wise man takes good care of it. Drink, friend! Drink to St John, and the Devil can do you no harm."

Tornefeld picked up his glass. "I drink," he said stiffly, "to my king, the Lion of the North, and his future conquests. His garden boasts a flower called 'the Crown Imperial'. May it long and gloriously flourish. I drink, too, to the health of all brave Swedish soldiers, of whom I am one no longer."

He drained his glass and hurled it at the wall with such force that it shattered.

The room had grown cold. The guttering candle-end on the table was on the point of going out. The miller rose and stretched.

"It's time," he said. "Now you must come with me."

They walked to the door together. The wind had ceased to howl, the air was crisp and clear, and the dark woods were gilded with moonlight. Tornefeld peered out into the night, looking for musketeers on their way to arrest him, but there was no one to be seen, only snow-mantled hills and dales and ploughland and moorland and trees and bushes and rocks, and, in the far distance, the lights of a lone cottage.

"Swear to me, friend," he whispered to the thief, "that you'll deliver the bible into my king's own hands."

"I swear it in the sight of God, friend," said the thief, with a sweeping gesture that embraced the night sky and everything beneath it. "I've always dealt honestly with you." But to himself he said, "The king is rich enough already – what need has he of such a sacred relic? I not only have the book, I have a use for it and mean to keep it. The Devil himself shan't take it from me."

They took leave of one another at the crossroads.

"My heartfelt thanks for your help, friend," said Tornefeld. "Fidelity still exists in this world. Farewell, and, if things go well with you, think of me sometimes."

On the edge of the forest the miller gave a shrill whistle and three figures emerged from the trees – three fellows whose

58

ferocious faces were scarred by fire. One of them laid a hairy hand on Tornefeld's shoulder.

"Who's this young popinjay you've brought us?" he demanded of the miller, roaring with laughter. "What are we to feed him on, milk pudding?"

"Remove your hand from my shoulder," Tornefeld told him angrily. "I'm a nobleman, and unused to such treatment."

"Nobleman or no nobleman!" cried the second man, and they both set about Tornefeld with their cudgels.

"Why beat me?" Tornefeld screamed in terror. "What harm have I done you?"

"This is just to make you feel at home," they told him, laughing, and proceeded to kick and thrash him through the forest to where flames licked the smelting-shed roofs and molten ore seethed in cauldrons.

The third man had lingered beside the miller. He pointed to the thief, who, without a backward glance, was bounding across a moonlit expanse of snow.

"He's making off," he said. "I've never in my life seen a man take such strides. Did he give you the slip?"

The miller shook his head.

"He'll not escape me," he said with a silent chuckle. "I'll see him again. He says he means to join the Swedish army, but he'll never get there. Love and gold lie in wait for him at the roadside."

PART TWO

The Desecrator

WITH GUSTAVUS ADOLPHUS' bible under his coat, the thief made his way through forest and scrub, across rocks and moorland, to where Black Ibitz and his men lay hidden in the so-called Fox's Earth.

He was not alarmed at the thought of having to steal past the dragoons on picket duty around their lair, for he had a thief's knack of rendering himself unseen and unheard whenever danger threatened, and the fox and the marten could have learned the art of concealment from him. No, what preyed on his mind was that he had promised that fool, Tornefeld, to deliver his arcanum into the hands of the Swedish king. He had no intention of so doing: the precious book hidden beneath his coat must remain in his possession. Because his conscience pricked him, however, he began to upbraid Tornefeld as if the youth were still walking at his side.

"Quiet, you dunderhead!" he growled angrily. "Why must you always open your mouth and wag your tongue? Catch flies with that beak of yours, but leave me in peace. I, join the Swedish army? If you're looking for a fool, friend, help yourself – there are folk enough hereabouts who covet a cap and bells. I don't give a fig for your king. If he wants the sacred relic, let him fetch it for himself – *I'll* not wear out *my* shoes on *his* account. I value my shoes, having procured them with my own five fingers, and he'll not present me with a new pair. Your king's a thrifty man – they say he counts all his army's picks and shovels for fear of losing a single one."

The thief paused to catch his breath, for the path led uphill. He readdressed himself to the absent Tornefeld as he walked on, but this time in a more conciliatory tone.

"Don't take it amiss, dear friend," he said, "but you've a stubborn spirit, God knows. You wish to pack me off to the Swedish army? What awaits me there? Four kreuzers a day plus cold and hunger, kicks and blows, moil and toil, hardships and battles, insults and drudgery – a dog's life, in other words. Well, I've enough pea-straw bread washed down with water soup – henceforth I mean to feast off brimming platters. My hour has struck, friend: I have the arcanum and I mean to keep it, no matter who tries to take it from me. What did you say? I swore on oath? I know nothing of that. Who heard me? Sir Nobody heard me, that's who. Well, where are your witnesses? You have none? You dreamed it, friend, I know nothing of any oath. What did you call me? A blackguard and a faithless rogue? That's enough, boy! I can see I shall have to crack your ribs before you're satisfied. Not another word, or I'll . . ."

He stopped short and strained his ears in the darkness: a horse had snorted somewhere close at hand. The dragoons! Silently, he dropped to the ground and wormed his way through the undergrowth with infinite care, inch by inch. Tornefeld had ceased to occupy his thoughts: he banished him from his mind for ever.

By daybreak he was in the Fox's Earth. In a clearing he saw a charcoal-burner's tumbledown hut and, standing guard outside the door with a musket in both hands, a man in a black Polish coat. A skinned hare hung from the doorpost. The two fires that burned in front of the hut cast a fitful glow over the frozen ground, and between them, sleeping wrapped in their cloaks, lay the bulk of Black Ibitz's men, for the hut was small and could shelter only a few of them. Two members of the band, who were awake, had skewered gobbets of meat on their knives and were holding them over the flames. A broken-down old nag stood tethered to a branch, eating its fodder from a nosebag.

For a while the thief lurked among the trees. One of the sleeping men stirred, called for brandy, and fell to cursing. The sentry on guard outside the hut propped his musket against the

64

door and chafed his hands, which were numb with cold. The pair beside the fire had removed the gobbets of meat from their knives and were cramming them into their mouths.

"*Benedicite!*" said the thief, emerging from the gloom. "Fall to, brothers. Enjoy your meal, but don't burn your mouths!"

They gaped at him. One of them sprang to his feet and gulped down the morsel in his throat, his eyes starting out of his head with alarm and exertion.

"Who are you?" he asked at length. "Did our sentries let you pass? Who sent you, the dragoons? Is the storm about to break?"

The man by the door, who had snatched up his musket, called out a belated, "Halt, who goes there?"

"Dear friend," said the thief, "I'm not from the dragoons. I heard of your plight and came to help you."

The man still seated beside the fire had been studying the thief's face intently. Now he rose.

"I know you," he said. "You're the Fowl-Filcher – you roam the countryside. What right have you to come here and talk so boldly?"

"I know you too," the thief replied. "You go by the name of Wryneck. We were once in Magdeburg Gaol together."

"I'm Wryneck, true enough, and this man here is Sainted Jonas. But now tell us: what ill wind brings you here?"

"You're up to your neck in trouble, so I came to help you," the thief said. "When the Bloody Baron attacks, I'll stand by you."

"You'll stand by us?" Wryneck hooted with laughter. "You fool! You're as out of luck as a fly in hot gruel. The Bloody Baron has a hundred dragoons and we're but twenty strong, with one horse and five muskets. We'll all be captured within the hour, God have mercy. How do you propose to help us?"

The thief chuckled. "What miserable, cowardly rascals you are. Even if the Bloody Baron had as many dragoons as leaves in the forest, I wouldn't fear him. He may have dragoons, but I have hussars. Where's your captain?"

The other robbers were awake by now and had got to their feet. They stood in a circle, staring with suspicion and bewilderment at the man who, armed only with a cudgel, was audacious enough to tackle the Bloody Baron and his dragoons.

"You have hussars?" exclaimed Sainted Jonas. "Fellow, you lie fit to topple the Tower of Babel. You expect us to believe that? May a thunderbolt strike you all, you and your hussars! Where are they? Where do you keep them?"

"Believe it or not as you please, it's all one to me," the thief rejoined. "They're lying hidden in the forest, waiting for me to fetch them. Where's Black Ibitz, your captain? I'm told he's a true man, a match for the Devil himself. I'd like a word with him. *He'll* not take fright at a whiff of powdersmoke."

"Black Ibitz is bedded down on straw in his hut," Wryneck replied. "He has the spotted fever and keeps calling for a priest. He wants to die."

The hut was filled with acrid smoke from a pan of smouldering pitch and juniper wood. Black Ibitz lay in the straw, breathing stertorously and tossing to and fro. Although he wore a sheepskin coat and red slippers like the king of hearts in a pack of cards, his black beard and bold, cruel cast of feature lent him a fearsome appearance even now, on the point of death.

A red-haired girl was crouching beside him in her shift, dabbing his forehead with melted snow and vinegar. Also in the hut were the surgeon and another of the band, a renegade friar named Feuerbaum. Having vainly searched for the dying man's gold in every nook and cranny, even to the extent of rummaging in the straw on which he lay, they were now urging him to confess and repent of his sins in the hope that he would, in his delirium, reveal where his thalers were hidden. So intent were they on their work that they failed to see the thief enter.

"Captain, Captain," lamented the surgeon, "you're done for. Death has already opened its jaws to devour you. You must go before God's throne and holy judgement seat."

"Your many grievous sins have aroused God's wrath," said Feuerbaum, raising his hands and smiting his breast like a priest intoning the Confiteor. "Receive Christ into your heart, my son, that the door of grace be opened unto you."

But nothing they said had any effect. Ibitz was so deaf to their entreaties that they might as well have blown on cold embers. The girl took a spoon and tried to coax a little muscatel between the dying man's lips. Feuerbaum launched into another homily.

"Praise the Lord that dwells in Zion," he said. "Will no pious word escape your lips? What use is your money to you now, Captain? You must leave it behind on earth and depart with only your sins for baggage."

At that moment, either because of the wine he'd swallowed, or because he'd heard money mentioned, Black Ibitz briefly recovered consciousness. He opened his eyes and groped for the girl, calling her his ewe-lamb and dearest sweetheart. Then his eyes sought the surgeon's face.

"Surgeon,' he demanded, "what time of night is it?"

"Your time is up," Feuerbaum broke in before the surgeon could reply. "Eternity beckons you, Captain, so direct your gaze toward God. You can hope for no mercy on earth, being so soon to enter the realm of Death, but God is compassionate. Confess, therefore, and acknowledge your sins."

"Eating meat in Lent when I was still a lad," Black Ibitz said in a low, mournful voice, "– that was the first of my sins."

But that was not what the surgeon and Feuerbaum itched to hear.

"You also stole, robbed, cheated, and amassed much property," Feuerbaum said accusingly, and smote his breast as if standing before the Eucharist in church. "For God's sake, Captain, be mindful of your salvation."

"Yes," Black Ibitz pursued, "I robbed and stole. I lived on the sweat and blood of the poor."

"So now confess where you hid their money!" Feuerbaum insisted. "Confess before it's too late, or you'll be lost to the Devil for ever more, body and soul. Confess!"

"No, you rogue, not to please the likes of you!" gasped Black Ibitz, sitting bolt upright. "Rather than tell you, you scoundrel, I'd sooner the Devil . . . ."

His voice died away. He had caught sight of the thief, who was standing in the doorway, and fancied in his delirium that the Devil had come to fetch him.

"There he is, there he is!" he cried. "Why didn't you keep a better watch on the door and window? Black Kaspar is standing there, ready to take me."

The girl saw the thief and dropped her spoonful of muscatel in alarm.

"Who are you?" chorused the surgeon and Feuerbaum. "What do you want?"

"I wish to speak with your captain," the thief began, but Black Ibitz, summoning up his last reserves of strength, had risen from the bed of straw and was tottering toward him in sheepskin coat and red slippers.

"Leave me be, sir!" he implored with frenzied gaze and chattering teeth. "I'm devout, I'm devout – I said three Paternosters but an hour since! There are others here in plenty, villains to a man, so why must I be the one to go?"

In mortal terror he flung open the door and pointed to his men.

"See, there are enough of them. Take them, they're yours. Take them, all of them, but leave me in peace!"

At that he again lost consciousness and collapsed. The girl dragged him back to his makeshift bed and wiped the sweat from his brow. The thief stood there, temporarily at a loss, then turned and went out, closing the door behind him.

It was light by now. The fires in front of the hut were going out and a pale, chill sun had risen above the pine trees. The thief drew his coat more tightly about him. He listened for a moment, but all was quiet inside the hut. Then he addressed the robbers who had gathered round him.

"You heard that. Black Ibitz appointed me your captain in his stead and bade me take you away from here."

The robbers murmured and laughed among themselves.

68

"You simpleton," one of them called out, "where will you take us, pray? To Onion Land, where fools grow wise and lambs slaughter butchers? Don't you know the straits we're in? The dragoons are upon us. How are we to escape them without horses? We're harried and exhausted."

"We shall make them welcome," said the thief. "Stand firm and fear naught. By the time we're done, not a man of them will wish to pursue us."

"Captain," said Wryneck, "why are you of such good cheer?"

"For a very good reason," the thief replied. "Mark this: I carry beneath my coat an arcanum so powerful that all I do must turn out well. Follow me, and good fortune will descend on you like manna from heaven."

"I, too, think it better to defend ourselves," cried Wryneck, already half won over. "If we surrender to the Bloody Baron, we'll end like sloes of which the cook says, 'One part boiled, one part stewed'. Those of us who aren't hanged will be branded on the forehead and sentenced for life to the Venetian galleys."

"If only we had sufficient muskets," said one of the band, "we wouldn't fear the Bloody Baron for all his power."

"What need have you of muskets?" the thief said laughingly. "A thick stick is better – it never misses. Mark this too: I don't consider the dragoons true soldiers. They can stand guard and dig trenches and build bridges – yes, they're masters with shovel and spade. When it comes to fighting, however, you'll find them fainter-hearted than old women."

"What of the hussars you made so much of?" Wryneck demanded. "Where are they?"

"Be patient awhile and I'll fetch them," the thief told him. Producing an empty poacher's sack from under his coat, he walked off and disappeared among the trees.

He returned with the bulging sack slung over his shoulder. He had previously, while walking through the woods, discovered a hornets' nest in a hollow tree not far away, and this was what the sack now held.

69

"Here they are, my little hussars," he said, holding the sack in the warmth that rose from the embers of one of the fires. "They'll soon be awake. Then they'll sing the Bloody Baron a song he never heard before."

A faint hum filled the air. The old nag tethered to the tree pricked up its ears, lashed out in all directions, and tried to gallop off.

The robbers, who had grasped what their new captain had in mind, were seized with enthusiasm. Eager to defeat the Bloody Baron and his dragoons in battle, they began to out-shout each other.

"We'll settle their hash!"

"We'll put them to sleep!"

"I'll douse the Bloody Baron's light for him!"

"We'll pick them off like wild duck!"

Just then a sentry came running out of the trees and announced that the dragoons, over a hundred strong, were riding across the fields from two directions. Another babble of excited cries went up.

"To arms, comrades! The enemy's at hand!"

"Slow-matches ready, muskets loaded with three balls!"

"Up and at them!"

"Aim at the belly, not the head!"

"I'll fire into the midst of them, then I'll not miss!"

"Be still!" commanded the thief. "Comrades, I'll go on ahead – I want a word with the Bloody Baron first. When you hear me say 'fox' – that's the signal – blaze away, and those without muskets fall on the dragoons with your cudgels. Now forward, and acquit yourselves like men. If anyone fears to join us, let him stay behind."

"With your permission, Captain," said Wryneck, "none of us will stay behind."

"In God's name, then," said the thief, and slung the poacher's sack over his shoulder.

The Bloody Baron was riding through the sparse pinewoods at the head of his advance guard when, in the pale, snowy light

70

of dawn, he caught sight of the robbers whom he had come to capture advancing toward him in a body along the forest path that led to the Fox's Earth. Although some of them carried muskets, he assumed that they were ready and willing to surrender on any terms. Unaware that they had taken new heart, he was about to spur his charger into a gallop and bear down on them when a voice hailed him from overhead.

"Stay where you are, sir! Ride no further or it'll end in tears."

The captain of dragoons looked up and saw a man perched high in the branches of a fir tree, swinging his legs as if he knew of no better place in the world. On his lap lay a bulging sack.

The captain rode up to the tree with his pistol cocked.

"Come down and let us see who you are, fellow, or I'll put a bullet through your hide."

"Why should I come down? I'm comfortable where I am." The thief laughed. "My advice to you, sir, is to wheel your horse and ride off. It would be safer."

"I know you now, fellow," cried the captain. "Of all the scoundrels God created, you're the most abject. I knew you were one of Ibitz's crew, but what I owed you yesterday I'll pay you today in good round coin. Choose the tree you wish to hang from."

"You're cooking your fish before they're caught," the thief said scornfully. "Heed what I say, sir – I mean you well. Retire in good time or you'll do so quicker than you care to."

Meanwhile, the main body of the dragoons had caught up with their captain and gathered around him, just as the thief had intended. He wanted them to form a solid mass.

One of them spurred his horse to the foot of the tree.

"Come down and let me flay you alive, fellow," he called. "I'll sell your hide to the regimental drummer for ten kreuzers."

"I'll shake you down, little man," shouted another. "I'll lay you across my shoulders and run to Hungary without pausing for breath."

71

"If you and your captain are so brave and strong," jeered the thief, "why don't you drive the Turks from Constantinople? I'm only one against many, but I warn you: spoon up your porridge too fast and you'll burn your tongue!"

"Damn your eyes!" thundered the captain, losing patience. "Come down from that tree!"

"Are you really so eager to be off, sir?" the thief said calmly. "I'm in no hurry. First I must bid your horse adieu."

"That's enough!" the captain roared. "Right wheel! Open order! Prepare to attack! And you, come down and give yourself up or I fire!"

And he raised his pistol and took aim at the thief while his men formed up for the attack.

"Let every fox look to his skin!" the thief cried, so loudly that the forest rang with the words: he had given his comrades the prearranged signal.

The captain fired, hitting him in the shoulder, just as he tossed the hornets' nest into the midst of the dragoons.

All that could be heard at first was a faint humming and buzzing. The dragoons cocked their heads and listened, not knowing what to make of it. All at once a horse leapt skyward like a jack-in-a-box. Another horse abruptly shyed and lashed out. Its steel-shod hoofs scythed the air and thudded into human flesh. There was a curse, an angry shout, and a scream of agony from the injured man. The captain, who guessed what was afoot, bellowed at his men to spread out, but his voice was quickly drowned by the pandemonium that erupted all around him.

The horses in the middle of the serried ranks tried to bolt when the hornets attacked them. They reared, plunged, and fell on top of riders pitched from their saddles. An indescribable din filled the forest: whinnies, cries of pain, oaths, conflicting orders, unheeded words of command, musket and pistol shots, and the reverberation of all this clamour. A disciplined body of men had transformed itself into a jumble of horseflesh and hoofs, of shouting, groaning, cursing dragoons who clung to their horses' manes or were dragged along by their stirrups, of carbine barrels and whirling sabres, of contorted faces and hands clutching empty air. Such was the turmoil into which the robbers emptied their muskets.

The dragoons were past holding, past taking orders. With or without their riders, horses scattered and careered off through the pine woods, soaring over bushes and undergrowth in their frenzied urge to escape. The few dragoons who struggled to their feet and tried to re-form were attacked with cudgels and musket butts.

The Bloody Baron, who now had his horse under control, wheeled it around in the hope of rallying his men, but it was too late: the robbers had already scattered them. Seeing that the day was lost, he spurred his charger into a gallop and rode off cursing. The thief bade him a mocking adieu from his perch in the tree.

"What, sir, no fond farewells? Why be off at such a breakneck pace? You'll lame your horse."

The battle was over. It only remained for the robbers to catch the riderless horses. The thief slid gingerly down his tree and stood leaning against the trunk. His wound was beginning to pain him and blood was seeping through his shirt and coat. In the distance, the Bloody Baron's trumpeter sounded the call to muster. Amid the pools of blood on the ground lay wounded dragoons, horses writhing in their death-throes, and pieces of broken harness, and littering the trampled snow, quiescent and numb with cold, were the true heroes of the hour: the hornets.

When the robbers had caught enough horses they mounted up, hoisted their wounded captain into the saddle, and rode back to the Fox's Earth with jubilant cries and much waving of hats.

The surgeon, who was standing outside the door of the charcoal-burner's hut when they reached the clearing, gaped at the sight of his comrades trotting along on horseback.

"A miracle!" he cried. "Is it really you? I'd never have believed it. The only way I thought we'd meet again was wolf-and-fox fashion, dangling from the skinner's pole. Dismount and we'll drain a glass together. Then take your spades and shovels. Black Ibitz is dead and in need of burying."

The thief stood in his stirrups.

"A Paternoster and an Ave Maria and God rest his soul, that's all we've time for. We must leave here at once. Those who wish to follow me, mount up; those who wish to remain here, remain."

The men began to mutter, but his angry voice quelled them.

"I'm your captain now, and I demand your obedience! The Bloody Baron is mustering his men for a fresh assault. We must go. You've seen for yourselves how swiftly the wheel of fortune turns."

At noon they halted at an inn not far from the Polish border, where they knew they would be safe. The thief lay stricken with fever in the hay-loft, the surgeon having bandaged his wound. Wryneck had remained at his side, but the remainder of his new comrades sat below in the tap-room drinking Polish brandy and making din enough to be heard a mile off.

"Captain," said Wryneck, who was crouching beside him in the straw, "are you really so sick? You groan as if your life were ebbing away."

"I've lost too much red gravy," the thief replied with a faint smile. "I'm sick enough. Were I sicker I'd die, no doubt, but I don't intend to do so. I mean to seek my fortune and I'll have it come what may. Even if it were chained to the firmament, I'd make it mine."

He tried to sit up, only to sink back into the straw.

"Those men carousing and feasting below," he said, "they're making a din like frogs in springtime, but fate is hard on their heels. They give no thought to the executioner's rope and wheel. We must leave here. Tell me the name of each and what he does best, and I'll tell you which of them will go with us and which remain behind."

"Me you already know," Wryneck began his tally. "My name is Wryneck."

"Yes," said the thief, "I know you. You were my companion in Magdeburg Gaol, where the bread was made of ground pea-straw. You'll come with me."

"And I'll be a good comrade to you," Wryneck assured him, "till the soul quits my body and I'm buried in barren ground."

"Go on, go on!" urged the thief. "Who's next? What is his name and what can he do?"

"There's Crooked Michel – he's good when it comes to a scrimmage. He can hold his own against any three men with pistol, sword and dagger."

"Shooting and sword-fighting only lead to trouble," the thief murmured. "Him I've no use for – him I'll leave behind."

"Whistling Boy," Wryneck pursued. "He can run well – he's as fast on his feet as any hare or hound."

"Let him run where he pleases, then, I won't keep him," the thief said firmly. "Cover me over with straw, I'm as cold as charity."

"Mad Matthes," Wryneck continued. "When it comes to wielding a sabre, he's the best."

But the thief's thoughts had strayed. The wound spell! If only he could remember the wound spell! Pain had gripped him again with such ferocity that he felt as if his life were draining away with his blood. There was a wound spell so magically powerful that it could staunch blood, but it eluded him. He racked his brains in a vain attempt to recall the words.

"Mad Matthes," Wryneck repeated. "He doesn't know the meaning of fear and will cover any retreat. Do you hear me, Captain?"

"Yes, I hear you," the thief said with his teeth chattering. "If he's ignorant of fear, he's ignorant of caution too. Let him go his own way – I've no use for him."

"Then there's Owlface, who needs no sleep. He can go without sleep for a week."

"What good is that?" the thief grumbled. "Don't you have anyone who can solder and file keys or take the imprint of locks in wax?"

"Feuerbaum," said Wryneck. "No lock is too strong for him and none too ingenious."

"Let him come with us, then." The thief emitted a faint groan. "It burns like fire!" he muttered to himself. "God forbid it should turn gangrenous . . ."

"Next, Veiland," said Wryneck. "He has ears like a fox. He can hear a horse whinny three hours' march away, dogs bark and cocks crow at two leagues, and people talking at once."

"He'll make a good lookout," the thief declared. "I'll take him with me."

"Before I forget," Wryneck went on, "there's Tinsmith Hannes. He's so strong, he can break down any door by charging it with his shoulder."

"That's no use to us," said the thief. "He'll only make a noise, and I'm no friend of noise. Can't you think of anyone better?"

"The Brabanter. He can disguise himself in a trice as a farmer, a waggoner, a grocer, or a student."

"He's the man for us, then," said the thief. "Good intelligence is always useful."

"He can also speak French," Wryneck added.

"Then he's salt on my soup," the thief exclaimed. "He shall teach me it so that I can pass for a nobleman."

"A nobleman?" Wryneck looked puzzled. "What do you mean? Is that the fever talking?"

"No, I'm quite myself," the thief replied. "That makes five of us, and five are enough. Go down and tell the other three –"

"But what of the rest?" Wryneck broke in. "What of Klaproth and Afrom and Red Konrad and Gallowsmeat and Sainted Jonas? We swore to remain together and never part."

"It's not for you to interrupt your captain," the thief rebuked him. "Your duty is to keep mum and obey orders. What you swore is your business, not mine. I don't want a multitude of men – I don't wish us to catch the eye like a covey of partridges in winter. Five fingers on one hand are sufficient for their purpose, so who has need of six or seven or ten? Besides, five are already too many when it comes to sharing."

Breathing heavily, for every word was an effort, he lapsed into silence. Wryneck, inspired by his talk of sharing, had been

76

smitten with an idea and couldn't keep it to himself.

"I know of a wealthy farmer not far from here," he began. "He has plenty of hams in his larder, and eggs and dripping, and wine in his cellar, and chests full of coin –"

"No," said the thief, feverishly turning on his other side. "I've no wish to break open farmers' chests and closets or burn and plunder villages. You're to leave the peasants to their honest toil."

"In that case," said Wryneck, "do you mean to lie in ambush by the roadside and prey on passing coaches?"

"No, not that either – I've something else in mind," groaned the thief, and clutched at his wound. "I mean to relieve the priests of their gold."

"Relieve the priests of their gold?"

"The gold and silver stored in their churches and chapels," the thief explained. "I seem to hear it crying out to be taken."

"I'd as soon be struck by lightning!" Wryneck exclaimed, aghast. "Robbing churches is sacrilege – it's a mortal sin."

"Listen carefully while I tell you something," the thief whispered. "Everything on earth belongs to God. The gold and silver in the priests' houses are His and will remain His, even when they're safe in our saddlebags. To my mind, it's a good deed to take unused treasures and distribute them among the people. But even if it's a sin, as you claim, you know this full well: it's as hard for a man to live without sinning at all, even on the best of days, as it is to make a coat without a yardstick and scissors or a house without masons and carpenters."

Wryneck nodded eagerly to signify that he had understood and was at one with his captain.

"Now go down," the thief went on, "and tell the other three to hold themselves in readiness to ride at midnight, and get me a cart filled with straw for me to lie on."

Wryneck set off down the stairs, and the red-haired girl, who had overheard every word, came out from behind a heap of straw.

"Captain," she implored, "take me with you and I will hold you as dear as my own heart."

77

The thief opened his eyes.

"Who are you?" he asked. "I've no need of you. Your hair is red, and I like neither cats nor dogs with fur of that colour."

"I'm Red Lisa, Black Ibitz's ewe-lamb, but now he's dead and I'm all alone in the world. Take me with you."

"No ewe-lamb can run with wolves," the thief told her feebly.

"This one can," said the girl. "Take me with you and I'll do any kind of work – spin flax, cook, launder clothes. I can also sing to the lute. I make warm gloves from hareskins, and for your wounds I have a salve compounded of fern and speedwell, plantain and checkerberry. Another ingredient is the flower called Devil's Bit. Half an ounce of that and one-and-one-half of the dog-nettle with the red flowers –"

"Keep the gangrene at bay, that's all!" groaned the thief.

"I'll banish the evil spirits that cause it to a desolate spot – I'll plunge them in water or bury them in a hollow tree," she promised. "I know the spell."

The thief gazed at her. "The spell?" he repeated in a hoarse, breathless voice. "If you know the spell, say it and I'll take you with me. The spell, in God's name, the spell!"

The girl thought for a moment. Then she began to sing:

> When Jesus in a circle trod
> all things began to weep.
> The leafy trees, the grassy sod,
> the . . .

"No!" the thief broke in. "That's not it. Say the other spell, the right one!"

"The right one," Red Lisa repeated. Laying her hand on the blood-stained cloth with which his wound was bandaged, she began to sing again in a low voice:

> Three flowers there grew . . .

"Yes," gasped the thief, "that's the spell, the right one. Go on, say it all!"

78

Three flowers there grew at God's behest:
one red, one white, and one, the best,
named by Himself "God's Will".
Blood, be still!

"Blood, be still!" the thief whispered. He closed his eyes, and it was as if the pain, having removed its murderous talons from his flesh, were soaring away on slowly, ponderously beating wings. Weariness overcame him, and he sank into a deep, dreamless sleep. His breathing became regular, and Red Lisa nestled against him in the straw like the ewe-lamb of her nickname.

The Desecrators, as they came to be known, ravaged the countryside between the Elbe and the Vistula for more than a year. They roamed far and wide in Pomerania and Poland, Brandenburg and the New Mark, Silesia and the Lusatian Mountains. Although malefactors had always abounded in those regions, no thief had ever dared to lay hands on the treasures of the Church, even in time of war and famine. Now that times had changed, people were horrified. They supposed at first that there must be more than a hundred robbers at work all over the countryside, plundering and profaning the holy places. Then, when it turned out that these outrages were being perpetrated by one small band a mere half-dozen strong, they promptly concluded that the Desecrators possessed the sorcerous knack of rendering themselves invisible in time of danger, and that it was hardly surprising if the Bloody Baron, for all his strenuous efforts to hunt them down, had never succeeded in capturing a single one. Indeed, many said that Satan, God's eternal foe, had taken personal command of them and made himself their captain in order to rob the churches and chapels of their sacred treasures.

The first to set eyes on this captain was the parish priest of Kreibe, a small Silesian village situated on the estate of a Herr von Nostitz.

One day in May after evening service, the priest, who kept

bees, went to the next village to agree a price for his honey with the grocer there. A sudden downpour compelled him to take refuge in the local tavern, so it was close on midnight when he returned to Kreibe.

As he was passing the church he saw a light in one of the windows, and for an instant the pitchy darkness was enlivened by the spectacle of St George, in his blue cloak, skewering a stained-glass dragon to which the village painter had imparted the appearance of a bat-winged cow in calf.

The light promptly vanished, but the priest now knew that there was someone inside the church. Although it contained two objects of appreciable value – a yard-long crucifix of solid silver and an ivory effigy of Our Lady crowned with gold, both of them votive offerings from Herr von Nostitz, who had recovered from the smallpox four years before – it never for one moment occurred to the priest that the Desecrators were at work. His only thought was of his two firkins of honey, which he kept locked up in the sacristy. This being the one secure place in the village, or so he thought, he stored them there in company with his smoke pot, bellows, and other beekeeper's implements.

The church door was locked, so he went to fetch the key, delighted by the prospect of catching the honey-thieves red-handed at last. Then, with a malediction ready on his lips and a candle in his hand, he entered the church.

The candle was extinguished by a gust of wind. He had taken a few more faltering steps in the gioom when the light of a bull's-eye lantern fell on his face and travelled down his cassock to his feet. The man in front of him was, he saw, pointing a pistol at his chest.

The malediction died on his lips. All he could muster in his fear was a whispered "Jesus Christ be praised!"

"For ever and ever, amen, reverend sir," the stranger said courteously. "If I alarmed you, please accept my apologies. I'm here at my own invitation, though I don't have the honour of your acquaintance."

Just then the priest discerned that the stranger was wearing a mask. He realised that he was confronted by one of the so-called Desecrators, and his blood ran cold. He was still staring at the masked man when the sacristy's heavy iron door swung open and three more men emerged with their faces similarly concealed. One was carrying the silver crucifix, another the Virgin's gold crown, and the third the priest's smoke pot and a bull's-eye lantern.

"How in God's name did you contrive to open that iron door?" he quavered, trembling in every limb, for the door had been well and truly locked, and he had only just fetched the key from his closet.

The masked man lowered his pistol and gave a little bow as if obliged to the priest for paying him the greatest of compliments.

"You should know, reverend sir, that to us iron doors are so many cobwebs to be brushed aside, nothing more. They trouble us not at all." He turned to his companions. "Hurry, we're pressed for time. Besides, we've no wish to incommode this reverend gentleman longer than is needful."

The priest saw the crucifix and the gold crown disappear into a large sack. As guardian of these hallowed objects, he knew that he ought to raise the alarm, cry murder, run up the stairs to the belfry and sound a tocsin loud enough to be heard for miles around. Being mortally afraid, however, he did none of those things; he merely stood there wringing his hands.

"Those are votive offerings from our gracious lord," he wailed. "Surely you wouldn't lay hands on *them*! His lordship presented them to God, not man."

"Not so," the masked man retorted calmly. "Only such part of his wealth as he gives to the poor is given to God. Everything else he gives to the world, and I am taking my share of it."

"But robbing a church is as grave a sin as any," the priest cried. "Return those sacred objects, or you condemn yourself to the uttermost depths of hell for all eternity."

"You should be less severe with sinners, reverend sir," said the masked man. "We all have need of one another. If there were no sinners and no sin, what use would anyone have for a parish priest?"

This robber captain was the Devil's mouthpiece, the priest knew it now, for only the Antichrist and Arch-Deceiver could bemuse a person with such smooth, insidious, pernicious arguments. He recoiled a step and hurriedly crossed himself.

"*Satana, Satana!*" he muttered in horror. "*Recede a me! Recede!*"

"What did you say, sir?" inquired the masked man. "I failed to catch your drift, not being a learned man myself. Latin is of little use to me in my profession."

"I said you were possessed by the Devil," the priest exclaimed. "He speaks through your lips."

"Not so loud, reverend sir, I beg you – someone might hear," the masked man said in a gently mocking tone. "If I'm possessed by the Devil, it was done by God's will and command, for not even a pig can be possessed by the Devil without His divine consent. I refer you to St Matthew, sir."

So saying, he turned and went over to his companions. The priest watched him go, wondering how best to describe him so that he might be recognised and arrested later on.

"Taller than most," he said to himself, "and lean of face, so far as I can tell. If only he weren't masked! A curly wig, a black hat and cloak trimmed with white. That's all, and little enough it is by way of a description . . ."

Meanwhile, the robber captain had taken the smoke pot from one of his comrades and was regarding it attentively. He rejoined the priest.

"I see you're a diligent beekeeper, reverend sir," he said. "How many hives, if I may be permitted to inquire?"

"Three hives," replied the priest. To himself, he added, "Slender hands such as are more usually found in persons of quality. Long, pickpocket's fingers, the chin clean-shaven . . ." Aloud, he went on, "I keep them in the meadow behind my house."

"Three, eh? They must yield eighteen or more measures of spring-gathered honey."

The priest sighed. "This year, ten-and-a-half measures only."

"That's very little for three hives," the captain said. "Yet it was just the kind of year the beekeeper craves: a summer with cool winds and heavy dews, a long, dry autumn, and a snowy winter. What was amiss?"

"Alas," the priest lamented, his thoughts flitting back and forth between his hives and the theft of his church's treasures, "my bees were afflicted with nosema."

"And you did nothing to cure it? You had no remedy to hand?"

"No," the priest said sadly, "there is none. One must simply let the disease take its course."

"Mark this, sir," the robber captain told him. "Wild thyme pounded up with a little oil of lavender and added to the bees' sugar-water – that's a proven remedy for nosema."

"I'll try it," the priest said thoughtfully. "But where am I to find wild thyme? I've never seen any in the fields hereabouts. Meantime, what of the honey? It refuses to clear. I've sieved it twice, but it remains as cloudy as before."

They were now alone in the church, the others having made off with their loot. The robber captain shook his head.

"That comes from the dampness in the air," he said. "The sacristy is no place for honey – the walls are streaming with moisture. Put it in the warmth of the sun, sir."

"I would, if it weren't for the peasants," the priest said plaintively. "They're such a bunch of thieves, they steal my honey at every opportunity. It's safe from them only in the sacristy, for I keep the iron door securely locked and bolted."

"So I discovered," said the robber captain. "It's a sorry thing when peasants are thieving rogues. Where property is concerned, each should attend to his own and refrain from coveting his neighbour's. But now, sir, I must bid you farewell and go."

They had been pacing up and down the aisle while speaking. The priest came to a halt.

"A pity," he said. "I've appreciated your company, sir."

83

"And I appreciate your saying so," the robber captain replied with equal courtesy, "but I must ask you to excuse me."

He bowed to the priest, blew out the bull's-eye lantern, and was instantly swallowed up by the darkness.

The priest lingered behind, debating where to keep his honey given that the walls of the sacristy were indeed streaming with moisture. Although it occurred to him after about a minute that he could now climb to the belfry and sound the alarm without risking his life, he thought it wiser to tiptoe after the robbers. Once he had seen where they went and whether they were mounted, he would summon the peasants and send them in pursuit.

But the Desecrators had gone by the time he emerged from the church. For all the moonlight in which the countryside was now bathed, not a sign of them could be seen in any direction. As he told the frightened peasants an hour later, it was as if they had borrowed the wings of the owl and the ravens that roosted in the church tower and flown away.

Unlike the parish priest of Kreibe, who escaped with nothing more than a fright, others unlucky enough to come upon the Desecrators at an inopportune moment did not always survive the encounter unscathed. One such was the verger of Tschirnau, a village on the right bank of the Neisse in the Bohemian county of Glatz, who surprised them just as they were making off. Their haul from this particular church, to which the peasants of the entire county made pilgrimage, comprised four silver candelabra, each six pounds in weight; a censer; a baptismal ewer and two patens, likewise of silver; a heavy gold chain; a piece of brocade embroidered with gold thread; and a book enumerating the charitable endeavours of Pope Martin V. The latter had been taken not for piety's sake but because it was encased in ivory.

"They'll all do nicely for the melting-pot," said a voice as the verger entered the church. He saw no one at first but the robber with the book in his hands. Then he caught sight of another two intruders. He was a brave man, and he knew that

84

the peasants in the nearby tavern would come to his aid if they heard a commotion. For want of any better weapon, he snatched the staff from a figure of St Christopher and brought it down on the head of one of the robbers, whose red hair caught his eye.

The red-haired robber cried out in a woman's voice. A moment later someone gripped the verger around the neck from behind, half-throttling him. He dropped the staff and strove to break his assailant's hold, but in vain. Just as the staff clattered to the flagstones, another man appeared in the doorway, masked like the rest, and gave a signal.

"He's alone," the man said. "There's no one following, that's why I let him pass."

The verger heard no more. A moment later he lost consciousness. When he regained his senses he was lying on the church steps bound hand and foot, his aching head swathed in a cloth, his eyes and lips sealed with plasters steeped in pitch. That was how the peasants found him on their way to the fields next morning, and beside him on the steps, broken in two, reposed St Christopher's staff.

A far worse fate lay in store for a young Bohemian nobleman who met the Desecrators at an inn between Brieg and Oppeln: the encounter was to cost him his life.

The inn, which stood beside the highroad in densely wooded country, was seldom patronised by anyone but gipsies and humble folk such as journeymen or, at most, a pedlar with his wares on his back. The young Bohemian count, who was travelling to Rostock with his tutor and a lackey, had been obliged to spend the night there because his carriage had sprung an axle. It was autumn, and the rain was teeming down outside. While the young count's coachman endeavoured to repair his conveyance, he and his tutor ate supper in the tap-room, waited on by the lackey. All the kitchen could produce was a small roast fowl and a pancake.

After supper the lackey went outside to assist the coachman. The tutor, being weary and in need of sleep, retired to the attic, where the landlord had made up beds for his two distinguished guests. The lackey was to sleep on a bench in the tap-room, the coachman in the stable.

The young count lingered in the tap-room over a jug of wine, alone except for an old man, the landlord's father, who lay snoring on the bench beside the stove. Rain pattered against the windows, blazing logs hissed and crackled, and pots and pans clattered in the kitchen, where the landlord's wife was preparing a supper of Nuremberg sausage for the coachman and the lackey.

The count, who had no wish to retire so early and hankered after a game of ombre, wondered if there were a couple of gentlemen of quality in the neighbourhood with whom he could play. He was debating this question, elbows on knees and chin in hands, when there was a commotion outside. He cocked his head and listened, fancying that he had heard one of his men, the coachman or the lackey, utter a cry for help. Just then the landlord came hurrying out of the kitchen, pale with fright. He was about to say something when the door burst open and a peremptory voice broke in.

"Messieurs! Stay precisely where you are."

The masked figure of the robber captain was standing on the threshold with three companions at his back, one of them red-haired.

The young Bohemian nobleman remained calmly seated behind his jug of wine. It occurred to him that, if these were indeed the Desecrators of whom he had heard so much, a cool head might not only save his skin but preserve the thirty Bohemian ducats he carried in his purse. Determined to emerge from this encounter with credit, so as to be able to boast of it later at the university in Rostock, he bolstered his courage by draining four glasses of wine in quick succession.

Meanwhile, the robber captain had entered the tap-room. He gave a little bow and raised his hat to the count, then called for wine and drank it out of a silver goblet which one of his companions produced from a saddlebag.

The landlord stood there trembling in every limb, so

86

frightened that the pitcher of wine nearly slipped through his fingers.

"What do you want?" he demanded with an effort. "I cannot give you shelter, as you must surely know."

"Fiddlesticks," the robber captain told him. "Be off with you. Hurry to the kitchen and see if there's some bread and fried bacon and small beer for my comrades."

Having draped his cloak over the back of a chair, he was now standing there in a shabby coat of purple velvet and turn-down riding boots. His companions had seated themselves at a table near the stove, all save the one with red hair, who remained at his side.

He turned to the young nobleman and raised his hat a second time.

"I regret that circumstances should have compelled me to intrude on you unannounced," he said courteously, "but the wind from Poland is bitter today, and I had no wish to abandon my companions in the freezing rain."

"A question, by your leave," said the count. "What has happened to *my* companions? I heard them cry out. And kindly remove your mask, sir, so that I may see your face."

The robber stared at him in silence for a moment.

"May God in his mercy preserve you from that sight," he said at length. "As to your servants, they've retired to the cow-shed, but never fear, my own people will spare no effort to serve your noble person in every respect."

And he indicated the two men sitting apart at their table.

The young count noted to his surprise that the captain of the Desecrators was at pains to imitate the speech and manner of a nobleman. He thought it wise to be equally polite, if only for the sake of the gold in his purse, so he rose, hat in hand, and invited the redoubtable man to join him at his table for a glass of wine.

The robber seemed to deliberate for a moment. Then he said, "In response to your courteous invitation, sir, I can only say that I consider myself unworthy of such an honour. If you insist, however, I'll gladly drink your health."

But it was Red Lisa who first raised her glass when the three of them were seated together at the count's table, and she drained it – as she had been wont to do with Black Ibitz – to the Devil.

"No blasphemy," the robber told her sternly, "you're in respectable company."

"The young lady wears male attire and carries a sword," the count began. "Is that the custom hereabouts?"

"No," the robber replied. "She dresses like a man because it enables her to sit a horse better, and the sword is no plaything – she knows how to wield it. When she draws it, she does so *pour se battre bravement et pour donner de bons coups.*"

"I myself have been to Paris," the count remarked, crossing his legs with a jingle of spurs. "I've seen the Louvre and the king's new pleasure palace."

"I cannot say the same," said the robber. "My French was taught me by my comrade there. It flows from his lips like water." He pointed over his shoulder at the Brabanter, who was seated at the other table with Wryneck, wolfing fried bacon.

"Will you be staying the night here?" inquired the count, anxious not to let the conversation flag.

"No," the robber replied, "I must ride on. I have business to attend to not far from here."

"In that case," said the count, "I'll drink to its successful conclusion."

"Kindly refrain, sir," the robber enjoined him. "If you wish a fisherman luck before he sails, he fails."

"How can you fail?" Red Lisa broke in. "You have the arcanum on you, and that will prevail over anything, however strong."

"Hush!" the robber said angrily. "You talk too much. I've told you often enough: what the mouth blabs, the neck pays for." He readdressed himself to the young nobleman. "My property is scattered about the countryside. To gather it in, I have to ride far and wide."

"And what form does your business take, sir, if I may make so bold?"

"You will divine its nature," came the imperturbable response, "if I tell you that I'm known hereabouts as 'the Desecrator'."

The count cast courtesy to the winds and jumped up. Although he had known from the first who the stranger was, it stung him to hear the truth so brazenly proclaimed. "Have you no shame?" he demanded, thumping the table with his fist.

"I feel neither shamed nor disgraced," the robber replied calmly. "If it has pleased Almighty God to make me what I am, how should a speck of dust like myself oppose His divine will?"

"Then it will also please God to have you hanged or broken on the wheel in due time," said the count, whose glasses of wine were beginning to go to his head, "and that will be the end of you."

"Not necessarily," the robber told him. "King David, too, was a great sinner, yet he died in great esteem."

"You have a slippery tongue, by heaven!" the count cried indignantly. "You make my head spin, you and your King David, but one thing's true, and I've often thought of it. Why didn't God make all men Christians? Why are there so many Turks and Jews in the world? It oughtn't to be so."

"Perhaps God has no wish to see too many people in heaven," the robber hazarded. "Methinks He would rather see them far away in hell than close to Him in heaven. What good can He expect of them? When men numbered only four they sought to kill each other, and they'll behave no differently up there."

"Enough of your preaching," said the count. "There are ten thousand reichsthalers on your head, and the man that brings you in alive will be granted a manorial estate."

"True enough," the robber conceded, "but know this, sir: the hare is never swifter than when hunted, and the net that will trap me has yet to be woven."

"Indeed?" cried the count, whose head was beginning to buzz with wine. "Well, I shall know you again when next I

89

see you. You're done for. The executioner's axe is hovering above your head like the sword of that ancient king whose name I've forgotten. My tutor knows, but he's asleep upstairs. Damnation, why wouldn't he play ombre? We could play three-handed now."

"You say you'd know me again?" the robber asked thoughtfully.

"Indeed I would, *par le sang de Dieu!*" declared the count. "What's more, I'll wager two Bohemian ducats on it."

"Two ducats are little enough," said the robber. "I accept your wager."

"Then the money's as good as mine," the count exclaimed with an exultant laugh. "I've an excellent memory for faces." And he reached across the table, quick as lightning, and snatched the mask of black cloth from the robber's face.

A sudden hush descended on the room, broken only by the clatter of Wryneck's knife as he dropped it on his plate. The robber captain stood up. The face he never wanted seen was pale and grew still paler, but his expression remained as bold and undaunted as ever.

"You've won your wager most commendably, sir," he said, smiling. "Here's the money."

He took two ducats from his pocket and tossed them on the table. The count picked them up and held them in his hand, palm upward. He seemed to have recovered his wits, as if a trifle alarmed by his own temerity.

"Now that it's time for us to part, however," the robber went on, "– time for me to go and you to stay – I think we should drink a farewell glass together for friendship's sake." He raised his goblet. "Your health, sir!"

"And long life!" the count added thickly. He raised his glass and put it to his lips, not seeing that Red Lisa had drawn a small pistol and shaken powder into the pan.

The shot rang out before he had emptied his glass. He sank back in his chair with a gentle sigh. The blood drained from his cheeks, his head sagged, his limp hands relaxed. The glass fell to the floor and smashed, the two coins went rolling across the room.

The robber captain stood there motionless for a while, inhaling the scent of powdersmoke. Then he picked up his mask.

"I wonder if he knew he had to die," he mused, glancing at the dead man.

"I think he knew it at the very last moment," said Red Lisa, "but I gave him no time to call out a 'Lord Jesus'. I'm sorry for him – he was a lively lad. That's not the end of it, though. I must prime my pan again, for there's another over yonder who has seen your face."

And she levelled her pistol at the old man on the bench beside the stove, who had awoken and was now sitting up, smiling foolishly.

The robber captain swiftly hid his face behind the mask.

"God have mercy!" he cried. "Isn't one enough? What am I to do with an old man? He became embroiled in this affair through no fault of his own. Am I expected to murder him?"

"Please yourself," said Red Lisa, "but if die he must, don't keep him waiting too long for the bullet. Fear is at its worst in the face of death."

"An old man," the robber captain groaned, " – how can I bring myself to murder an old man? I cannot, but what's the answer?"

"I'll do it for you if I must," Wryneck told him, "but give the landlord a coin for the burial and the saying of a Mass."

"He cannot be left alive," the robber captain said at length, "though it comes hard, God knows. Summon the landlord, one of you."

The landlord crossed himself on seeing the dead man. When he heard that his father, too, must die, he went down on his knees, begging for mercy and beating his breast.

"It's no use," the robber captain told him. "I'm sorry, God knows, but he must die. Go bid him farewell."

"What harm has he done you?" the landlord wailed. "Take pity on him. Is your heart so hard that nothing will dissuade you? He's my father. Were I not so wretchedly poor, I would ransom him from you."

"It's a misfortune," said the robber, deeply moved by the landlord's lamentations, "but the thing has happened and cannot be undone. He saw my face, which I ordinarily conceal behind this mask. I cannot ride off and leave him alive."

The landlord got to his feet. He looked at the old man seated on the bench beside the stove, who was staring into space as if he had no notion of what was going on around him.

"How *can* he have seen you," the landlord protested, "when he has been blind as a mole these twelve years past? I even have to guide his spoon to the plate, yet you claim he saw your face."

He slumped into a chair, buried his face in his hands, and began to laugh with wild, shrill abandon.

The robber captain stood there in silence for a moment. Then he went over to the stove and, in one swift movement, thrust his pistol in the old man's face. There was no reaction; not a muscle even twitched. The rheumy eyes remained fixed on a shadowy corner of the tap-room.

"He's truly blind!" the robber exclaimed, and lowered his pistol. "I'm absolved, heaven be praised! Enough of that laughter, landlord! Your father may live, and I'm glad of it." He turned to the others. "And now, mount up. We've wasted too much time as it is."

The landlord continued to sit there, still laughing.

As soon as the robbers had ridden off, the landlord returned to the tap-room to find his father crawling about on all fours.

"Well," he demanded, "*did* you see his face? Cease your antics. On your feet and tell me. You're blind no longer."

"Now that I'm rich," said the old man, rising slowly to his feet, "I'll not share my wealth with you. You've always kept me short of food and clothing, never treated me as a good son should. I told you so often enough, but –"

"You saw him?" the landlord broke in. "You'd know him again?"

"No," mumbled the old man, "I had no time to look at him."

"You had no time? What the devil do you mean?"

"I had no time to look," the old man repeated stubbornly. "I awoke when they shot him" – he indicated the dead youth – "and the pieces of gold went rolling across the floor. They're mine now, for I watched where they went and took care they didn't escape me. One of them I saw disappear into a crack in the corner, so that one I was sure of, and another rolled toward me under the bench, so I quickly put my foot on it and didn't budge. There may have been three, though. I must go on looking."

"Who cares if there were twenty, you old fool!" the landlord shouted. "We've lost ten thousand reichsthalers, don't you understand? It never comes twice in a lifetime, a stroke of good fortune like that!"

Furiously, he slammed the door behind him and went to fetch the coachman and the lackey from the cow-shed so that they could keep vigil over their master till morning.

The Desecrators undertook their last robbery on the Monday after Passion Sunday in spring of the year 1702. The place was a church near Militsch celebrated for the heavy gold cross above the high altar. The venture misfired because the parish priest, on his bishop's advice, had some weeks earlier removed the ancient crucifix to Militsch Castle for safekeeping and replaced it with a wooden Christ of mediocre workmanship.

The robbers were seen climbing empty handed out of the church window by a farmer who had risen in the middle of the night to tend a sick cow. Without stopping to dress, he ran to Bafron Manor in his nightshirt and raised the alarm. Herr von Bafron, who was still awake and sitting at cards, mustered such of his people as were to hand or could be speedily summoned: farmhands, charcoal-burners, household servants, and huntsmen.

They were too late, however. As soon as they knew themselves to be in danger, the robbers had followed their usual procedure and scattered to the four winds, each making for the Polish border by a different route. Thus, although their pursuers patrolled every road and combed every wood in the neighbourhood, not a member of the band was intercepted. All that came to light was a sack dropped by the robbers in the course of their headlong flight. It contained some bread and onions, a small bag of coarse salt, and several molars wrapped in a cloth – presumably relics from some previously-looted church.

Next morning the Bloody Baron arrived with a detachment of dragoons from his quarters in the little town of Trachenburg. Having four months earlier returned to Silesia from fighting the Turks in Hungary, he had promptly resumed his campaign against the robbers with all the perseverance of a bloodhound. He flew into a rage on being told that a mendicant friar in a brown habit had been detained not far from the Polish frontier but subsequently released, for he knew that one of the Desecrators had sometimes employed that disguise. The only person he himself encountered on the road that day was a Swedish courier riding toward Trachenburg at dawn with his official leather pouch. This man, who addressed him as "Cousin" and exchanged a few words in Swedish and French, had impressed him as wholly unsuspicious because envoys from the King of Sweden were to be found on every road in Silesia and Pomerania.

Such was the outcome of the Desecrators' last robbery, and nothing more was heard of them until, some time during the week after Easter, the rumour first arose that they were no more.

Somewhere in the Polish forests – so the story ran – they had quarrelled while sharing out their spoils and set upon each other with knives and muskets. Three of them were killed on the spot and the survivors had ridden off into the blue with their stolen gold. Among the dead was their leader.

The rumour spread like wildfire. Waggoners proclaimed it in passing to reapers at work in the fields, parish priests wove it into their sermons, and there were some who claimed to have seen the robbers' corpses with their own eyes. Everyone was overjoyed that the deplorable state of affairs had been brought to an end, and the robber captain's wretched demise became the subject of a printed ballad sung at fairs and in taverns.

But there was one person who refused to believe the tale, namely, the Bloody Baron, who scoffed at it and called it an imposture. The robbers, he declared, had put it about that their leader was six feet under the sod. Why? So that people would give up looking for the man and leave him to enjoy his ill-gotten gains in peace. The Bloody Baron swore by the Devil's claws, tail and horns that he would never rest and never know a day's peace of mind until he had marched the Desecrators and their captain to the gallows.

Nothing more was heard of them, however. No more churches or chapels were robbed, and such of their treasures as remained intact continued to gleam and glint in the many-hued twilight admitted by their stained-glass windows. No thieving hand was ever laid upon them.

The Desecrators had a secret lair, a hut in the wooded mountains of Bohemia known as the "Sieben Gründe", and it was there that they assembled for the very last time.

It was early in the morning and still cold. The wind whistled through chinks and cracks, and a thin drizzle was falling outside. Four of the band lay wrapped in their coats on the straw, gazing with red-rimmed eyes at the glittering heaps of coin in the centre of the hut: the thalers and double-thalers, the Kremnitz and Danzig ducats which back-street receivers of stolen goods had paid them for the proceeds of their past year's depredations in Bohemia and Poland.

The council of war had lasted all night. Reluctant to let their captain go, they had shouted and bickered for hours. Their store of gold was still insufficient, they argued, and there was plenty more to be had for the taking. All their arguments were in vain, however: the captain insisted that they must part.

"We ply a trade," he told them, "a trade in which all must

95

sooner or later pay the price with neck and crop. Have a care! Unless we keep a bridle on our tongues it won't be long before we feel the touch of the hangman's noose. Besides, the Bloody Baron has returned, and I've no wish to encounter him again. That's why I say we must part or our luck will desert us. Each of us must go his own way without a backward glance at the others. Such is my command, and you swore to obey me in everything when I saved you from the gallows."

That settled the matter. It only remained for them to divide the larger of the two heaps of coin among themselves and go their separate ways.

The captain was standing outside the hut in his worn and faded coat of purple velvet, intent on the days that lay ahead. He would use the wealth he had amassed to pay off the debts encumbering the Kleinroop estate, purchase farm implements and breeding stock, engage new workfolk, and stable good horses for the mail coaches that passed by. "A greyhound and a saddle-horse, too, for the young lady who is to be Herr von Tornefeld's high-born bride!" he told himself with a smile. "After all, there's no lack of money now."

Inside the hut, meanwhile, Red Lisa was bending over the smaller heap of gold and silver coin – the captain's share – and filling his valise with double-thalers and ducats. Feuerbaum had risen, unable to watch any longer. The sight of money destined for another hurt his eyes.

"What the devil!" he exclaimed. "Is everyone free to take as much as he pleases?"

"What's it to you? That's the captain's share," Wryneck told him sharply. "By rights you should thank him for leaving you as much as he has. When he joined us you had neither clothes nor shoes – a threadbare habit on your back was all you possessed, but he has brought us good times. Henceforward you're a wealthy man."

"Wealthy?" the renegade friar cried indignantly. "What are you saying? Who's wealthy in these ruinous days, when a bushel of corn costs eleven groats and a half? I shall leave my share untouched – I'll save it against my old age, for no one

96

will help me when I'm lame and palsied. Till then I shall have to depend on God's mercy and beg dry crusts at farmers' doors to keep from starving. *That's* how low I've sunk – *that's* my reward!"

And, with a bitter laugh, he took the share which Wryneck thrust at him: a hat brimming with thalers and a handful of gold.

"We risked life and limb to get that gold," said the Brabanter. "Now I propose to enjoy a lengthy rest from my labours. I shall live in luxury. Elegant lodgings at some comfortable inn, a good table with fish and roast meat every day and the proper wine to go with them. Morning Mass, an afternoon drive in my carriage, and a game of cards in the evening. That's how I propose to live, peacefully awaiting whatever the future brings, good or ill."

"Ah," Feuerbaum broke in shrilly, "but what if your luck runs out? What if you end by starving in the gutter? When that day dawns, don't come to me. Not a copper will you get from me, friend, I tell you that now, so don't come hobbling up to *my* door!"

"Never fear," replied the Brabanter, quite unruffled. "You may plant lilies and mignonettes outside your door, I'll not trample them."

Wryneck had received two handfuls of minted gold because he was the captain's second-in-command. Now it was his turn to speak.

"We've lived like night-owls, unable to show our faces by day," he said, "but that's all over now. I've a fancy to ride through all manner of countries – Venice, Spain, France, the Netherlands – and see the world in broad daylight. And if I spend only two thalers of my money in the week and a half on Sundays, it'll last me till my life's end."

Veiland, a big, burly fellow with a pallid face, let the ducats trickle through his fingers and chuckled to himself.

"Here in Bohemia, where not a soul knows me, I'll have a goldsmith make me a cup and a knife, a ladle and a snuff spoon of solid gold, likewise two little snuff boxes of gold, one for my right pocket and one for my left. The one in the right pocket will be for me, and the one in the left I'll offer my friends, for thrift is a virtue."

"And you?" Wryneck called to Red Lisa, who was squatting silently on the ground. "Why look so wretched when you can live in silk and velvet? Is your heart heavy? If a man's feet itch, let him go. One sweetheart follows hard on the heels of another, you should know that by now. When you've gold buckles on your shoes and necklaces and combs and rings and bangles of gold as well, your admirers will be legion."

Red Lisa made no reply. She rose and tried to pick up the captain's valise, but it was too heavy, so Wryneck had to help her carry it outside. There she made a last attempt to shake her lover's stubborn resolve.

"Take me with you," she pleaded, resting her forehead on his shoulder. "Don't tell me 'No!' a second time. I know that you've given your heart to another. She may be more beautiful than any woman under the sun, but no matter, take me with you notwithstanding. I'll not get in your way – I'll gladly sleep beside the stove in the servants' quarters and do the worst of work provided I know where you are in God's world and how you're faring."

"It cannot be," the captain replied, cold and unbending. "Look for a dry pebble in the sea, but don't come looking for me. You'll never find me in a thousand years."

Red Lisa wept awhile. Then she grew calm again and wiped the tears from her eyes.

"Farewell for ever, then," she said quietly. "I've loved you as dearly as my own heart. Leave me, and may God preserve you wherever you go."

Meanwhile, Veiland and the Brabanter had emerged from the hut. They bade their captain a boisterous farewell, cheering and firing their pistols in the air until the forest rang. And when he spurred his horse and rode away with a final wave, Veiland tore off his neckerchief and burned it to the captain's health and continuing good fortune.

★

98

One week later Feuerbaum was trudging along the Silesian highroad in his friar's habit. He had buried his money at three places in the forest and marked the trees to help him find it again. Now he was roaming from village to village, farmstead to farmstead. His beggar's satchel contained some bread and onions, three sour apples, a small piece of cheese, and, wrapped in a cloth, a tuft of hair which he passed off as a sacred relic.

While tramping the dusty road in this way he heard a horseman come trotting up behind him. He turned his head to see a Swedish courier in blue tunic and brass buttons, elk-leather breeches, a belt of buffalo hide, and a plumed hat. He promptly stepped aside and proffered his open hand as the horseman passed by, though with little hope of alms, for the Swedish king's officers seldom dipped in their pockets when they saw a mendicant friar.

This time, however, the horseman reined in. A smile flitted across his face, and he tossed the friar a Pomeranian half-guilder.

Feuerbaum caught the little silver coin, but an instant later he straightened up with a jerk and stared.

He knew that mocking smile, and those eyes that blazed like a wolf's, and the bushy eyebrows that met above the nose, and the furrow in the brow. Surely it was his former captain who sat looking down at him from the saddle?

"Is that the most you can spare an old comrade?" he cried, seizing the rider's arm. "I knew you at once despite that little beard you've grown. Come down from your horse, and if you've a drop to drink on you . . ."

He fell silent, for the smile had left the rider's face. A wholly different person looked down at him – a complete stranger – and a voice he had never heard before addressed him in broken German.

"What amiss, friar? Half-guilder not enough? Out my way, or I beat you hard!"

Feuerbaum stared at the unfamiliar face for a moment longer. Then he threw up his hands in dismay and called God to witness that he had mistaken the high-born, worshipful gentleman for someone else, he couldn't imagine why. The courier cut him short.

"Those are *excuses misérables!*" he snarled. "I no wish to hear. Half-guilder not enough? Out of my way, damned cur!"

The renegade friar obediently leapt aside and the horseman rode on. All that could be heard was a mocking laugh which Feuerbaum again found familiar. Wide-eyed and open-mouthed, he gazed after the Swedish cavalier until he disappeared from view, repeatedly crossing himself with a tremulous hand as if he had just encountered the Devil in person.

PART THREE

The Swedish Cavalier

IT WAS EARLY AFTERNOON when the Swedish cavalier reached the deserted mill.

The sun stood high in the cloudless sky and a summery hush enveloped the countryside. Not a breath of wind was stirring, not a bird chirping. All that broke the silence was the song of the crickets and the low, organlike hum of the bees. A gaudy butterfly disported itself amid speedwell, cardamine and dandelion. In the far distance, where the bishop's forges and smelting furnaces lay, a pall of black smoke hung over the pine forests.

The Swedish cavalier saw it and was assailed by a faint sense of unease, as if it held some danger for him, but he dismissed the notion with a shake of the head before it had properly taken shape. Then he dismounted and tethered his horse to a willow tree so that it could graze in a circle.

The door of the miller's house was locked. No smoke rose from the chimney, and the shutters were closed. The erstwhile miller, whom he had once, at an evil hour, mistaken for a ghost arisen from the grave, a poor soul from Purgatory, must be whipping his team along some highroad on the way to fetch merchandise from distant lands for his master the bishop. Even if his waggon came rattling up the hill at this moment, who would fear him now?

The Swedish cavalier sat down in the tall meadow grass and stretched his legs. Resting his back against the brickwork of the miller's well, he daydreamed with half-closed eyes.

He recalled how, poor and wretched and numb with cold, he had made his way to the mill through waist-deep snow, and how he had there acquired the arcanum, the key to his good fortune. Well, now he was a grand gentleman with plumes in his hat and money and letters of credit in his pockets – now he could proudly pass for one of the nobility. Let the miller come, him and his crooked mouth! Purgatory was a fiction, not a real place – it existed only in priests' heads, so he had been assured by the Brabanter, who had travelled far and wide and been wherever folk broiled bacon over coals.

He gave a start. What was that sudden hubbub? To hear it, one might have fancied that Venice had fallen into the hands of the Grand Turk. What did the unseen people want, and what were they shouting? A multitude of voices both deep and shrill, they came from all sides, from far and near, and their cry was always the same: "Make haste! Make haste! Make haste!"

What manner of people were these, and what did they want? The Swedish cavalier looked about him, but there was no living soul to be seen except his horse, which was standing beside him munching heather, toothwort and tufts of grass, and nothing to be heard – no cries, no shouts – save the hum of the bees.

He leaned back against the brickwork and let his head loll forward on his chest. There it was again! Sometimes near, sometimes far, sometimes soft, sometimes swelling to a mighty roar, the multitude of voices cried "Make haste! Make haste! Make haste!"

He tried to rise, but he could no longer do so. Something took hold of him, lifted him, bore him higher and higher, and still the thunderous, tumultuous voices around him cried "Make haste! Make haste! Make haste!" Then silence fell.

He found himself high in the sky, surrounded by turrets and battlements of cloud so bright and dazzling that his eyes could scarcely endure it. Covering his face with his hands, he peered between his fingers and saw three men seated on thrones with steps leading up to them. They wore long, fur-trimmed robes and red shoes, and one of them, a stern-eyed youth, he recognised as St Michael, the heavenly chancellor, whom he had often seen in effigy. Before the three stood an angel of gigantic stature with a drawn sword in his hands, and surrounding them in serried ranks was the heavenly host whose earlier cries of "Make haste, make haste!" had, it seemed, been a summons to see justice done.

"*Votre très humble serviteur,*" murmured the Swedish cavalier, bowing and doffing his hat with a flourish, nobleman fashion, in a show of respect to St Michael, his scales, and his celestial associates, but none of the three judges so much as glanced at him. Now that silence had descended on the heavenly host, the angel with the sword raised his mighty voice.

"Michael and you fellow judges twain, I ask you now: is it the day and the time to sit in judgement?"

And the three men in the long robes answered as one:

"Since the Supreme Judge deems it time, it is time."

The angel with the sword looked up at the dazzling vault of Heaven.

"Almighty Lord," he cried, "is the court duly met?"

From above, like a tempest lashing an oak forest, came the voice of the Supreme Judge.

"The court is duly met. If anyone has a charge to bring, let him bring it."

From the heavenly host came a whispering and rustling of wings. Then silence returned. The Swedish cavalier experienced a sudden pang of fear. "What am I doing here?" he asked himself, plucking awkwardly at his blue tunic. He was looking around for some means of stealing away when he perceived that all eyes were upon him. The silence was broken by the angel with the sword.

"This man whom I have summoned before the court," he declared, "stands accused of having been, for many years, a thief. He robbed peasants' larders of bread and sausage and eggs and dripping and whatever else he could lay hands on. I charge him with that crime before God's court, once, twice, and thrice."

"Is that the extent of his wrongdoing?" said the long-robed man seated at St Michael's right hand. "A morsel of bread, an egg, and a little lard are difficult to procure on earth by honest means."

"He was so poor, he owned nothing but his shadow," said the judge on St Michael's left, and St Michael himself, Heaven's chancellor, fixed the Swedish cavalier with a stern eye.

"Who," he said, "would rebuke the pauper in his homespun smock for turning thief when the rich amass their wealth by unjust means?"

"He is innocent and may go his way in peace," the Supreme Judge declared from on high, his voice as gentle as the strains of a harp.

"God be praised!" the Swedish cavalier whispered, wiping the sweat from his brow. "All honour and glory to His holy name."

"God be praised!" the heavenly host chimed in on every hand. "All honour and glory to His holy name!"

But the angelic swordbearer remained where he was. Gazing at St Michael and his fellow judges with furrowed brow, he waited for silence to fall once more.

"There's more," he said. "I charge the same man with having, for the space of a twelvemonth, been a robber of churches. He stole their silver plate, their censers and patens, chalices and candlesticks, ornaments and reliquaries of gold, and now he means to use them for his own well-being and prosperity. I charge him with that crime, once, twice, and thrice."

"Yes, I did that, God have mercy," groaned the Swedish cavalier, glancing fearfully at the archangel. "God have mercy!" intoned the heavenly host.

"Gold and silver," said the first of St Michael's fellow judges, "are the cruel weapons and devices of the Evil One on earth. We have naught to do with them. They are not ours."

"They are not ours," the second judge repeated. "They are the objects of man's vain folly. An Ave Maria said in all humility is worth more to Heaven than any gilded pomp."

"They are not ours," St Michael ordained, and directed his gaze heavenwards. "When He trod the earth, He possessed neither gold nor silver. What is to be done with this man?"

"He is innocent," the Supreme Judge proclaimed from the luminous heights above. "He is innocent and may go his way in peace."

The Swedish cavalier breathed a sigh of relief. "I never knew," he murmured to himself while a mighty "Benedicamus Domino" arose on all sides, "I never knew that poor sinners were so leniently treated here above. That angel there, the one with the sword, he always gets the worst of it – I'm glad I'm not in his shoes. The trial is over, so why does he linger? What more does he want?"

"The trial is far from over!" the angel with the sword proclaimed just then. "That man you see muttering to himself – that, justices of the celestial court, is secretly of so wicked a disposition that he shamefully betrayed his comrade in adversity, a Swedish nobleman, and duped him by forswearing himself. Woe unto him and woe again, once, twice and thrice!"

The angel's loud accusation was succeeded by a lengthy silence. Then the first of St Michael's fellow judges spoke.

"That," he said in a voice fraught with sorrow and dismay, "is a grave and pernicious sin deserving of careful consideration."

"How could he have betrayed a companion in misfortune?" the second judge complained. "Had the divine spark in his soul been extinguished?"

St Michael shook his head. "Much has been said," he observed, "but none of it may be true." He rose and turned to the angel. "Accuser, where are your witnesses?"

"Yes indeed, where are they, your witnesses?" whispered the Swedish cavalier, torn between fear and hope. "Where do you propose to find them, accuser, since no one else was present?"

"My witnesses are ready and waiting to be examined," replied the angel with the sword. "Make way for them. They are many."

The heavenly host drew back at his signal, forming a wider circle. The angel called down into the depths:

Heath and meadow, marsh and sand,
highways, byways, fallow land,
wind and snow and reed and sedge,
fire and water, gate and hedge,
wayside stone and cottage too,
come before us and speak true!

At that the mute witnesses, the earthly things, ascended from below with a deal of rumbling and creaking, grating and grinding, hissing and roaring, and the celestial judges understood their language.

"The witnesses have been examined," the angel cried above the din, "and have testified. The accused stands indicted of iniquitous conduct."

"He is guilty," the Supreme Judge thundered from on high. "Accordingly, I sentence him as follows: he shall bear the burden of his sins alone for as long as he lives, never acknowledging or confessing them to another soul, only to air and earth."

The Swedish cavalier was seized with fear and trembling. He knuckled his temples in despair, and terror transfixed his limbs. The heavenly host lamented and wept all around him – indeed, even the angel with the sword was moved to pity.

"Almighty Lord," he cried, "that is too harsh a punishment. Can he hope for no pardon?"

"For him there can be no pardon," the thunderous voice replied from on high. "I entrust him to you upon your oath and honour. You are commanded to execute my sentence."

The angelic swordbearer obediently inclined his head.

"Then I will take this man," he said, "and set him down once more on the grassy heath . . ."

The Swedish cavalier stretched and rose. He stretched again, rubbed his eyes, and untethered his horse.

"If it wasn't a dream," he told himself as he rode down the hill, "I need no longer fear the wrath of God. He wished my previous existence to remain a secret, what else? Well, so do I, for it would be foolish of me to tell folk who I was and what I used to do! The Last Judgement is another matter altogether. There's such a blaring of trumpets on Judgement Day, so it's said, that a person's ears are deafened, but I never heard so much as a single wail from a bagpipe. No, it was nothing but a phantasmagoria, a dream."

All that struck him as odd and inexplicable was that he should have been so horrified in his dream when forbidden to tell anyone about his past life. This puzzled him, but he had no time to ponder the question because another source of concern was preying on his mind.

The grain in the fields on either side of him, as he rode along, was gloriously ripe and golden. The soil had been well manured and the seed-corn sown at the proper time, the ears were heavy and the farmhands working with a will wherever he looked. Behind the reaper came the sheafer, behind the sheafer the binder, and behind the binder the sheaf-carrier.

"This landowner rules his workfolk with a rod of iron," the Swedish cavalier told himself with an aching heart. "Things aren't as they used to be – I've come too late. The young lady has married, and her husband, the new lord of the manor, knows how land should be managed. My luck has deserted me even before it changed for the better."

Further on, however, when he came in sight of the thatched village and, beyond the maple trees, the slate roof of the manor house, the fields all around were in their old sorry state. Weeds of every kind – brome-grass, vetch, cranesbill, and field-madder – were growing up between the stalks, and the ears were coated with a black, powdery substance which showed that the seed-corn had been unripe, the time of sowing ill-chosen, and the soil poorly dressed.

The Swedish cavalier straightened in the saddle and spurred his horse into a trot.

"No!" he thought exultantly. "The estate has no new master – she's still unwed. She fell on such hard times that she was forced to sell off fields and meadows to her neighbours, that's the answer. All she has left is the land around the manor house itself. I'm in time, thank heaven."

Now that he was to see her again, his heart leapt like a wild stallion. He stood waiting in the garden, and all the flowery phrases he had rehearsed fled his mind when he saw her tripping along the gravelled path in her dainty red morocco shoes. His one thought was that all his dreams and daydreams had come true, and that this moment had decided his fate. For the first time, he trembled with fear at the thought that she might recognise him. Her erstwhile greeting rang in his ears: "Where do you hail from, you poor man? Quickly, go down to the kitchen and have the maid crumble you some bread in a bowl of soup . . ."

Summoning up all his courage, he went to meet her with his hat beneath his arm, bowed, and simply stood there. Now was the time for him to speak, but he could not utter a single word, and it was she that spoke first.

"You must pardon me for having kept you waiting, sir. They told me only just now that a stranger wished to call on me. I was not in the house, you see. I had to shoo the fowls from the garden, they do it so much harm."

Yes, that was the voice that had once pleaded for his life. The Swedish cavalier stood there entranced, all eyes and ears. She was as lovely as a summer's day – the Devil himself would have called down a blessing on such beauty.

"Custom prescribes that a third party should introduce you to me, I suppose, *mais je ne tiens pas à l'étiquette, monsieur.*"

"Would you repeat that, *mademoiselle?*" he said, awaking from a kind of dream. "My knowledge of French is only passable. I had no competent tutor in my boyhood, so the language leaves my lips more readily than it enters my ears."

The girl stared with a touch of surprise at this nobleman who so freely admitted that his French was not of the best and made no effort to pose as a fashionable gallant.

"You are an officer, sir?" she asked.

"Indeed I am," he said, slapping his scabbard, "an officer of the Swedish Crown at the service of God and all good folk."

"Have you come far?"

"I'm fresh from the ranks of His Majesty's cavalry. I took part in sundry battles, too, without meaning to boast of it. Now, however, I've renounced a soldier's life."

"And what brings you here?" asked the girl, unable to account for the stranger's presence.

"Since my journey brought me this way, I could not forbear to pay my respects."

"I'm truly *reconnaissante*, sir," she said, looking down at her red shoes in some confusion.

For a while they stood there, at loss for something more to say. The garden exhaled a scent of tuberoses, carnations and jasmine. Nothing broke the silence but the distant creak of a draw-well.

"This is not my first visit to your estate," the Swedish cavalier said at length in a hesitant voice.

"Ah, yes," the girl replied after a moment's thought. "In my father's time we received guests here every day, many officers among them. Now, however, we live more modestly."

"I was distressed to learn that your ladyship's father had departed this world," said the Swedish cavalier. "He was often in my thoughts, being my godfather."

"My father was your godfather?" she exclaimed in surprise.

"Yes, and I have a little ring given me by yourself. I treasure it."

The girl had gone deathly pale. She clasped her breast and drew a deep breath.

"I implore you, sir," she said in a whisper so soft as to be scarcely audible, "tell me who you are."

"I had hoped that you would know me again," he replied haltingly, huskily, his throat constricted with fear. "If you could but recall the day we drove down the hill and the sleigh overturned because the horses bolted . . ."

A cry transfixed the air. An instant later, racked with sobs and trembling in every limb, she flung herself into his arms.

"Christian!" she cried exultantly.

"None other," he said, and at that moment he truly became the Christian von Tornefeld whom he had banished to the bishop's inferno. His hand stroked her hair with infinite tenderness, and his lips shaped the name he had heard only once before and never before uttered.

"Maria Agneta," he said, and she raised her blissful, tearstained face to his.

As they strolled hand in hand along the gravelled paths and grassy walks, intimately conversing with many a "Do you still remember?", the Swedish cavalier felt an urge to embrace the very sky. It was as if he had abandoned the gloomy wilderness of his past and emerged into a sunlit meadow.

They came to a mossy bench overlooked by a nymph of weather-worn sandstone with a timid, melancholy smile on her face. Here he paused, pensively surveying the fragments of a cloven-hoofed faun lying strewn across the grass. Maria Agneta rested her head on his shoulder and pressed his hand.

"Yes," she whispered, "you haven't forgotten. It was here beside the little heathen god that it happened."

"It was indeed," he said, not knowing what she meant. His uncertain gaze roamed from the faun's horned head to the bench and the nymph and back again.

"We swore that the love in our hearts would never fade," she went on, "and you, Christian, told me, 'I'll never forget you any more than I can forget my Maker.'"

"Those were my very words," he assured her firmly.

"In the dark days that succeeded my father's death," she said as they walked on, "those words were my only source of hope and consolation. I thank God with clasped hands that you're here at last. You kept me waiting a long time, Christian."

"I too have known dark days," he told her. "I've tramped the dusty highroads and slept under many a hedge in rain and snow, but that's all behind me now."

"You would soon have found me gone. I must leave here and earn my bread by laundering clothes and tending children."

"Laundering clothes and tending children – a high-born lady like yourself?" he exclaimed in surprise and dismay.

"Yes, or I must spin and weave. I cannot remain here on the estate."

"And why," he demanded, "can *ma cousine* not remain here on her estate?"

"I'm poor now," she replied. "My means are exhausted. Herr von Saltza, my godfather, owns everything: the roof over my head, the bed in which I sleep. He has my notes of hand, and he keeps urging me to marry him." She broke off. "Christian, your freckles! Where have they gone? Now I know why I didn't recognise you at first."

"I believe I remember this Herr von Saltza," he said quickly. A vision of the fork-bearded man took shape in his mind and then faded. "Do I take it that *ma cousine* has no wish to marry him?"

"How can you ask me such a thing, Christian!" she replied in a faintly reproachful tone. "I'd rather sleep on oaten straw like a peasant girl than share a swansdown bed with my noble godfather."

"My dearest," he cried, exultantly, taking both her hands in his, "have no fear of Herr von Saltza and your notes of hand. Send for them, I'll redeem them. How much do they amount to in all?"

"I cannot say," she replied. "My bailiff has them recorded in his ledgers. I was forced to sell fields, pastureland and the fish pond, though I don't know how it came about. There was never any money in the house."

"How could it have been otherwise!" he exclaimed with such a wild peal of laughter that she recoiled in alarm. "There's not one honest man on your estate, did you know that, *ma cousine*? The bailiff, the clerk, the shepherd – they're a band of unhung thieves, *ma cousine*, and that's why they fail to keep order among the workfolk. Everyone here does as he pleases, didn't you know?"

"But how do *you* know it, Christian?" she asked.

"I inspected the fields yesterday, *chemin faisant*, and they're a pitiful sight. I also came here at dawn today, while *ma cousine* was still asleep. There was much to see. The clerk keeps four cows of his own and feeds them on your after-grass, did you know? The stableman and the cowman breakfast on omelettes and fried bacon washed down with buttermilk, when their rightful fare is pea, turnip or cabbage soup. The reapers go off to work in the fields with a whole cheese or three dozen eggs or a duck and sell them in the village over yonder, and the bailiff has perforce to turn a blind eye because everyone on the estate knows of his own dishonest dealings. And that's the fellow whom *ma cousine* appoints her overseer and pays through the nose to boot!"

"All this is new to me," Maria Agneta said humbly. "My guardian, Herr von Tschirnhaus, who has known the bailiff since his childhood, says he's honest."

"*Sans doute*," the Swedish cavalier declared with a scornful laugh. "He was honest while he lay in his cradle, never since. But that's not all. The barns and stables . . . Those holes in the roof! The rain gets in, the fodder rots, and the consequence is cattle-fever. This is the season of the year to sow millet and plant cabbages, mow grass and make hay, yet none of those things has been done, *ma cousine*, did you know?"

"You must speak to the workfolk, Christian. You must show them you're resolved to change things."

He dismissed her suggestion with a wave of the hand.

"Talk does no good, it only parches the throat. I shall have to thrash them into obedience and honesty – I'll restore order with a rattan cane in my fist." He swung round abruptly. "You there, fellow! Haven't you learned to salute your betters?"

Startled by this rebuke from an unknown gentleman, a passing farmhand whipped off his greasy cap and bowed low.

"Go find the bailiff," the Swedish cavalier commanded, "and, when you've found him, tell him that her ladyship requires him to bring his books to me and render an account of his dealings. He may await me upstairs in her ladyship's dining-room."

★

It was two hours before the Swedish cavalier returned to the garden. Maria Agneta ran to meet him.

"I've never in my life worked harder," he told her, drawing a hand across his brow. "I'd rather brave rough roads for a week in wind and snow then endure all that again. The bailiff's scribblings have spoiled paper enough to keep every cheese-monger in the Holy Roman Empire supplied for two years, but his ledgers make no mention of his having taken a fifth part of your wool and every fourth churn of your milk, day in day out. With *ma cousine*'s permission, I sent him packing. He's gone."

"You must do as you think fit," she said. "Your wishes are mine."

"When every debt has been settled," he went on, "I shall still have enough to pay for the priest's ministrations at our wedding, and the musicians, and your wedding dress, and a wedding breakfast for the neighbours – provided, of course, that my wishes and yours are alike in this respect too."

"Christian," she said softly, "I've waited so long for you and for this moment. Now that the time has come, I give myself to you gladly. I've loved you, you alone, all my life."

He bowed his head, and for an instant, despite himself, his thoughts returned to that other man, that lost soul whose name, freedom and honour he had taken for love's sake.

"Nowhere on God's earth," he went on, "will *ma cousine* find a man who loves her as dearly as I, and that's the truth, so help me God."

"I know it, Christian," she said with a smile.

"But there's another thing I must tell my dearest bride-to-be," he said. "I shall have to work like a Trojan, and we shall both have to share our peasants' black oaten bread for a long time to come."

"I'll eat black oaten bread with you, Christian," said Maria Agneta, "and I'll thank God for showering me with such happiness."

★

One night two months before her confinement, when it was already past midnight, Maria Agneta awoke and lay musing, unable to sleep. She could feel the child stir within her – the child that would be named Maria Christine if it was a girl, and it was a girl she wanted most. In her dreams she could already see her little daughter running across the farmyard in a white taffeta gown and a black and white bonnet, and when she became entangled in her gown and fell the peasants laughed and ran to help her up, and even the geese and goats in the farmyard laughed too. Lying there with her eyes closed and a smile on her lips, Maria Agneta surrendered to the thoughts that ran through her head. A year ago the presses had been empty of linen and napery, but now all was as it should be, for the house had a master once more. Thanks to God, the giver of all good things, her fortunes now reposed on firm foundations. She loved her husband beyond measure and could hardly wait for him to return from his long hours in the fields. At eventide, when she heard his step upon the stair, joyous expectancy made the blood pound in her temples. Now he lay sleeping at her side. She raised herself a little and listened. He was breathing peacefully, but there were nights when he led so turbulent a life in his dreams that he groaned and flung his arms about and cried aloud. On such occasions, or so she surmised, he was back with his king in the Swedish army.

Everyone, villagers and neighbouring gentlefolk alike, called him "the Swedish cavalier", for he never wore any coat other than the blue Swedish officer's tunic in which he had first arrived at the manor – indeed, there were some who ridiculed him for shunning the sunlight because it showed up the darns and patches in that threadbare garment. He was for ever scrimping and saving on the grounds that there must be money enough in the house for the christening feast, but she, Maria Agneta, had secretly purchased a length of blue velvet – at a half-guilder the ell – from a Polish Jew bound for the fair at Leipzig. Though determined that people should see him in a new coat, she was afraid to tell him so. Once, when she had said that a nobleman should look the part, he retorted, "Every cooper and carpenter struts about these days in silk and velvet, so the true nobleman should spite them by wearing a peasant smock."

"What kind of a nobleman is he?" the village folk murmured. "When he has a foal, a calf, or a sheep to sell, none knows better than he how to bargain. He'll haggle over a kreuzer with a commoner, so where's his nobleman's dignity?" He merely laughed when told of this. "What use have I for a nobleman's dignity?" he said. "Dignity never fattened cow nor sow."

Despite this, Maria Agneta reflected, her Christian was an officer and a gentleman *sans reproche.* He made her a new *déclaration d'amour* every day, and she loved to hear him call her his sweetheart, his little angel and dearest treasure. At the same time, he had to work hard to provide them with the necessities of life. Too pressed for time to join his beloved wife at the luncheon table, he would take a bowl of gruel with the farm-hands. During the day he had to be everywhere at once. "The master of an estate," he often said, "must acquaint himself with every straw that fills the crib and every shaving that falls to the ground in the wood-yard."

Although Maria Agneta yearned to be truly of help to her husband, she found it hard to remember all he taught her. She knew how much kindling and firewood must be brought into the house daily, and how many quarts of beer were consumed at Sunday dinner, and when the workfolk were to be given meat or millet or milk soup or gruel or flummery or dumplings, and that the dumplings must be made of rye and barley flour in equal parts, but she knew many more things besides, and she repeated them softly to herself to pass the time, just as Christian had told them to her.

"The landlord in the village shall have two brace of chickens and three dozen eggs every month. In return, his wife shall weave eleven pieces of linen for the manor. When I was little the villagers got up a Twelfth Night play and the landlord played Balthazar, but he had to be one of the shepherds, too, and play the bagpipe. A jet-black shepherd he was, and he couldn't scrub the soot off his face. How I laughed! The village blacksmith shall have eleven guilders' worth of iron and eight bushels of wheat for keeping the ploughs and other implements in repair – he has a little boy of nine to work the bellows for him. The trees in the pastures belong to the manor, so the miller has no claim on them. They're elms and oak trees, and the oak, Christian says, is a good tree – a tree from which hams and sausages can be plucked. The village women are duty-bound to work in the farmyard for a kreuzer a day and their food. A sheep yields a pound and a quarter of wool per shearing, a wether a pound and a half. Before I forget, I must tell the shepherd tomorrow that he's to keep his hens in his cottage and not in the sheep-shed. A sheep yields . . . How much does a sheep yield per shearing? Why can't I see the moon any more? There must be a mist again. March mists aren't good, Christian says – they bring hail-storms a hundred days later. The clock just struck one. It's long since I lay awake so late. It was one o'clock at night when they brought the Lord Jesus before Pilate, and Peter stood in the courtyard and warmed his hands over the fire. How cold I am!"

She drew the bedclothes over her shoulders, and as she lay there in the dark, vainly awaiting the advent of sleep, she was suddenly overcome with melancholy and dread. She fancied that she was alone in the room, and that Christian was far away and in terrible straits, crying out for help with flames dancing all around him. So lifelike was this vision that she herself could have cried out in fear and despair. Although she knew that he was peacefully asleep beside her, she found herself mourning him as if he were gone from her for ever. "What is this?" she asked herself in dismay. "I'm suddenly plunged in melancholy, but why, why? He's here beside me – no, he's far away and crying out for help with no one to hear him. Forgive me, God, it isn't true. I shouldn't have said that – it's not right – but what ails me? Why should I feel so afraid?"

She slipped out of bed, picked up the tinder-box with trembling hands, and lit the wick of the copper lamp. Its flickering light fell on the face of her sleeping husband. She gazed at him as he lay there with his hands folded on his chest, and the fear within her refused to ebb. It seemed to her that there was something strange about his still and motionless face, something she had never seen before – something from another world – but what it was she couldn't tell.

A shiver ran down her spine and she began to weep until the tears fell thick and fast.

"He isn't gone," she whispered to herself. "He's here with me, but – God forgive me – I fancied for a moment that a stranger was lying at my side. How could such a thought have entered my head, and why should I persist in weeping now that I can see him? Why, why?"

She looked again at the sleeping man's face, hoping that the sight would calm and console her, but the longer she looked the heavier her heart became.

And then, in her dire distress, she was struck by a sudden thought: she remembered that Margret, formerly a chambermaid at the manor, had taught her how to converse with a person asleep. "Make the sign of the cross over him," Margret had said, "and take him by the left thumb. That will give you power over him. Then call him in the name of God and ask what you wish to know, and he must tell you the truth willy-nilly."

"Forgive my foolishness, Christian," she whispered. "It's only a game – only because I want to prove Margret a liar, and because you happen to be asleep while I'm awake. She told me many tall tales, did Margret, before she ran off with the soldiers – for instance, that you can see the Devil riding through the air if you anoint your eyelids with bat's blood, but that's not true, someone tried it and saw nothing. If I do this thing, it's only to pass the time. Forgive me, Christian, but the night's so long and I cannot sleep."

Very swiftly, she drew the sign of the cross on his brow and took hold of his left thumb.

"Who are you?" she asked with bated breath. "Tell me who you are! In the name of Almighty God, answer!"

At that, the sleeping man's face turned pale and his breathing became as laboured as if his chest were weighted down with stones. His mouth shaped some words, but he choked them back and clenched his teeth as if two men were wrestling within him, one eager to speak and the other – the victor – resolved to prevent it. All that emerged from his lips was a groan.

"In the name of Almighty God," Maria Agneta cried despairingly, and she turned away rather than dwell on that stranger's face. "If you are not my Christian, why did you come here – why did you say you loved me?"

There was a moment's silence. Then, in the slow, muffled voice of one dreaming, the answer came:

"In the name of God, I came because I've always loved you. It happened when first I saw you – I couldn't help myself."

"Christian!" she cried, surprised and overjoyed, for who but he could have spoken of bygone days? Even as she watched, he opened his eyes and drew a hand across his brow. And when, still half asleep, he sat up and saw her and put his arm around her shoulders, his face had resumed its old, familiar appearance, and her fears and misgivings were as swiftly dispelled as a troubled dream fades at the moment of waking.

"My little angel," she heard him say, "there are tears in your eyes. What's amiss?"

"It's nothing," she whispered. "Truly, dearest, it's nothing. I was weeping, I don't know why, but it's over now. Sometimes, you know, tears are a sign of happiness."

"Go to sleep, my darling," he told her. "You must sleep, it's very early yet."

"Yes," she whispered, overcome with weariness and already half asleep. Gently releasing himself from her embrace, he smoothed her pillow and reached across her to extinguish the lamp. As she sank back, her hand sought his once more and her eyelids dropped.

That was the only occasion on which the true image of her childhood sweetheart arose in her mind. From that night forward, becoming fused with the image of the man she had married, it never returned.

★

Her pains began on the Wednesday after Easter, while she was walking across the village green with a pound of bread for the old errand-woman, who could no longer walk. She just had time to hurry home and prepare herself.

Her husband, who had to be summoned from the fields, was hailed as soon as he rode into the courtyard and told that it was a girl.

The christening was attended by all the local nobility. The Üchtritzes, the Dobschützes, the Rottkirchs, the Bafrons, the Bibrans, the Nostitzes from Bohemia, the Tschirnhauses from the Electorate of Saxony – all converged by carriage or on horseback.

That afternoon the manor house was filled with guests. The ladies sat in a room on the ground floor nibbling preserved fruit and pastries and sipping aquavit. The only one of them to keep the young mother company was Barbara von Dobschütz, a sharp-nosed old lady much given to expatiating on her devotion to God and good works, though she did so in her own peculiar manner, rebuking the Almighty in the tone she ordinarily employed to a servant who had displeased her.

"I'm often so pressed for time, my dear," she complained. "There's the sermon to be listened to on Sundays, and one day a week of bible study and another of prayer and penitence, and alms to be distributed, and the sick to be visited, and an hour's devotional reading every afternoon – why, this year alone I've read the *Garden of Paradise* and the *Celestial Wreath of Honour* three times over from beginning to end. Ah yes, one does one's best to satisfy the Almighty, but He too often treats His devotees in the strangest manner, to say the least. I went down on my knees . . ."

The Swedish cavalier had silently entered the room and tiptoed over to the bed. He laid his hand on the white lace cap that covered Maria Agneta's brown curls.

"My sweetest angel," he said softly, "I came to see you and the little one. You're thin in the face, but lovely as a summer's day."

". . . down on my knees," the old woman pursued, "and

prayed to Him to deliver me from rheumatism this year, but what good did it do? Instead of rheumatism, I now have the migraine. Ah, my dear, the agonies I've suffered . . ."

The Swedish cavalier bent over the cradle.

"You see, my God-given darling?" he whispered to Maria Agneta. "Her little fists are clenched – she's asleep." And he left the room as silently as he had come, closing the door behind him.

The old woman sighed. "If He treats others as He treats me," she said, still speaking of the Almighty, "He should not be surprised to find all His churches empty ere long."

The table in the great dining-hall was thronged with gentlemen seated over jugs of wine and bottles of Rosoglio, Spanish bitters and Danzig brandy.

The Swedish cavalier had withdrawn to a window alcove with Melchior Bafron, who was reputed to be the best husbandman in Silesia. There they conversed on the properties of good and bad soil, on the profit to be had from renting pastureland, on how calves should be tended and how difficult it was, at the present time, to make money out of fattening pigs.

"Speaking for myself," said Melchior Bafron, "I've always been more in favour of raising cattle. Pigs can lose you a mint of money – there's nothing worthwhile to be expected of them till they're lying on the butcher's block. Cattle, on the other hand . . ."

His host was not entirely in agreement.

"All livestock can lose a man money if he fails to tend his beasts properly," he said. "A pig's twelve bushels of inferior grain should be no cause for regret. What I get for bacon after twelve weeks' fattening makes an agreeable entry in my account book."

Meanwhile, conversation at the dining-table had turned to current events and the imminence of hostilities. It was rumoured that the young King of Sweden, now in Poland with his army, planned to march through Silesia and wage war on the Electorate of Saxony.

"So we shall soon be afflicted with epidemics and rising prices," sighed Baron von Bibran. "Foreign armies always bring such evils in their train."

"It wouldn't hurt us were the price of grain and cattle to rise," Herr von Dobschütz objected. "The King of Sweden pays well enough."

"Yes," old Tschirnhaus chuckled, "he pays well in quotations from the Gospels."

"Even were Poland and Saxony to join forces," young Hans Üchtritz cried eagerly, "they would never withstand the Lion of the North. He'll bring the Elector of Saxony to heel just as he imposed terms on the King of Denmark."

"Your health, Hans!" came the deep voice of Herr von Nostitz, Hans's brother-in-law. "Your very good health, but I tell you plainly, if I were the King of Poland I'd as soon have the Devil for a neighbour as Charles the Swede. At least I can cross myself and send the Devil back to hell."

"Hush!" said his cousin, Georg von Rottkirch, from across the table. "Have you forgotten where you are? Being a Swede by birth, our host will naturally side with his king. Do you mean to pick a quarrel with him?"

"I said nothing amiss," protested Herr von Nostitz, who liked to live at peace with everyone. "A man can cross himself before the Devil, but not before an ill-disposed neighbour, that was my only meaning. I seek no quarrel."

"At home, where the couriers change horses," young Tschirnhaus reported, "one hears all manner of things. It's said that the King of Sweden means to double the nobility's term of service with the colours and levy one peasant in seven. It's also said that he means to wage war on the Samoyeds who dwell in the snows beyond Moscow."

"He'll wage war for as long as he can find enough able-bodied men," said Baron von Bibran.

"I consider him an envangelical hero, a present miracle and an example to future generations!" Flown with wine, young Hans Üchtritz bellowed the words so loudly that the copper chandelier above the table vibrated in sympathy. "I raise my glass to the King of Sweden's victory and everlasting renown!"

The others frowned, reluctant to join him in such a toast, and did so for their host's sake alone. His was the only voice that broke the ensuing silence.

"Against the colic," he was saying, "I give a piglet brick dust mixed with a little oil."

Young Üchtritz silently replaced his glass on the table. Herr von Nostitz sat back in his chair and laughed till his wig wobbled. Just then the door was flung open and one of the farmhands, got up in livery for the occasion, announced a belated guest, Baron von Lilgenau.

The others jumped up and clustered around the new arrival. Nothing could be heard at first but a confused hubbub. Then Herr von Nostitz's deep bass voice drowned the rest.

"Hans Georg, my friend, where have you sprung from? It's a year since I saw you last."

The Swedish cavalier had likewise risen to his feet.

"I had no knowledge of her ladyship's betrothal and marriage," he heard the newcomer say. "Then, as I was riding by, someone called out that a christening feast was in progress. I leapt off my horse at once and ran up the steps. Where's Tornefeld? I must make his acquaintance – I knew his father."

The Swedish cavalier felt as if an icy hand had clutched at his heart. Walls, guests, jugs of wine, the table – everything in the room was spinning like a top.

"Herr von Tornefeld," he heard Nostitz say in a kind of dream, "allow me to present Hans George Lilgenau, captain of dragoons, a friend of mine and eager to make your acquaintance. He's cousin to the Lilgenaus of Mankerwitz."

"Welcome, sir," murmured the Swedish cavalier. The ground quaked, the glasses danced, the chandelier swayed. He kept his feet with a supreme effort. His one thought at that moment was of Maria Agneta lying abed in her chamber. It was all over.

For the second time in this house, he was face to face with the Bloody Baron. The voice of his mortal enemy rang in his ears.

"I knew your father, the Colonel," said Lilgenau. "I was privileged to fight under his command at Saverne."

Saverne? Was it a trap? Saverne, Saverne . . . When and where had he heard of the place before? Of course! It was at the mill, when Tornefeld had said, "What would you know of Saverne and how things were there?"

"Ah, yes," he replied, drawing a deep breath. "My father often told me of Saverne and – how did he put it? – 'the thunder and lightning of battle, the cries of "Advance!" and "Retire!", "Rally!" and "Charge!"' It was at Saverne that he lost an arm."

The Bloody Baron looked at him long and hard.

"It's almost laughable, how closely you resemble your late lamented father," he said, and the festivities resumed their course.

Whenever the harvest was good, the Swedish cavalier purchased a few more acres from his neighbours – a field here, a meadow there – to add to his original three hides of land. Now that five years were up, he had recovered all the land dissipated for his own profit by the former bailiff. But the lord of the manor took no great pleasure in food and drink, nor did he ever linger long beside the hearth. At every season of the year he would be out in the fields as soon as the Angelus bell had rung, watching his farmhands while they reaped and sheaved, dunged the soil and dug ditches.

Good husbandry provided an ample living for his family and his workfolk alike. His cattle multiplied, his woodlands became a source of revenue. The store-rooms were filled with all that a great house required, the coach-houses contained sleighs and carriages large and small, the stables were always ready with fresh horses for the mail coaches and couriers that called at Kleinroop Manor, and people came from miles around to admire the Spanish rams in the sheep-shed.

Sometimes, however, when he was riding across the fields with the land that belonged to him stretching away on either side, a shadow flitted across his soul and a chill like a night wind smote his cheek. It was as if all that he considered his own – the fields and pastures, the scattered birch trees, the grain burgeoning in the fields, the stream flowing through the water-meadows, the house and estate, the wife he loved and the child he so anxiously cherished – as if all this were not his own but lent him for a short while only and destined to be taken away, and the more brightly the sun shone, the darker his mood became. On such occasions he would wheel his horse and ride home like the wind, and when his horse's iron-shod hoofs struck sparks from the gravelled courtyard and his little daughter came running out of the garden, Maria Agneta would capture her, and, with a radiant smile, hold her up for him to embrace and fondle from the saddle.

It was only when his arms were about the child, a creature of flesh and blood, that the shadow lifted from his soul.

He loved his wife as dearly as he had loved her from the first – his affection for her was proof against the all-consuming ravages of time – but his love for little Maria Christine, his daughter, was fiercer still and tinged with painful unease. Hers was the face he looked for first on coming home, and his eyes lit up with enduring joy at sight of her.

Sometimes, when he had spent all day in the fields and returned home late, he would tiptoe to Maria Christine's bed-side and sit there in silence, listening to her breathe. Not that he meant it to, the intensity of his gaze would obtrude on the little girl's dreams and wake her. She would sit up pouting and close to tears, and then, seeing her father, fling her arms around his neck. To earn his release he had to sing her some nursery rhymes – always the same ones, for he could remember very few. He sang of the wolf on Shrove Tuesday, and of the Angelic Host, and how the tailor stood at Heaven's gate, and how the beggar man celebrated his wedding, and of the hen that refused to lay any eggs. "Strike it dead, strike it dead! It lays no eggs and eats my bread," sang the Swedish cavalier, and the hen would come fluttering over the edge of the bed in search of crumbs, and the Shrove Tuesday wolf that didn't care for meat lay idly at the little girl's feet, and the tailor and the beggar man pranced among the chairs, and Herod peered through the bedroom window. Herod came from the Twelfth Night Song, which Maria Christine liked best of all, and she often began it herself in a piping treble.

> Kaspar, Balthazar, Melchior sweet,
> King Herod's beard grows down to his feet . . .

Then the Swedish cavalier would add his deep voice to hers, and the two of them would sing so softly that no one else in the house could hear.

> Swiftly they rode over hedges and stiles,
> in seven hours five hundred miles.
> When Herod's palace came in sight
> the king looked down and shone a light.
> "Kaspar, Balthazar, Melchior, stay!
> Whither away, friends, whither away!"
> "We ride as fast as any wind
> the Virgin and the Child to find."
> "Kaspar, Balthazar, Melchior fine,
> bide and take a brandy wine."
> "Nay, ride we must, an it you please,
> to Bethlehem, the place of peace."

"Thy countenance is ever bright . . ." Maria Christine's little voice began, but that was from another song altogether. Sleep descended, muddling her thoughts until it was all she could do to keep her eyes open. Her father rose and tiptoed to the door as quietly as he had come, and after him flitted the strange creatures that had briefly populated the room: the wolf, the chicken, the tailor, the beggar man. Last of all to disappear was Herod of the long beard.

It was March, in other words, that season of the year when "the thread on the distaff snaps", as the peasants say, meaning that work in the fields must begin. The light was fading, snow clouds were scudding across the sky, and crows cawed harshly in the still leafless maple trees. Upstairs in the manor house, the Swedish cavalier was pacing the Long Room while Maria Agneta sat beside the fire studying the copperplate engravings in a compendium of garden flowers, her brown hair tinged with red by the glow from the blazing logs. The village schoolmaster was seated near the window with Maria Christine, endeavouring to teach her the art of spelling, but the little girl kept peeping at the corner where her wooden toys, a horse and cart, lay temporarily discarded. Standing between the door and the table, cap in hand, were two men from the village: a tenant farmer come to beg some seed-corn, and the carpenter, whom the Swedish cavalier had summoned to discuss the building of a new grain loft above his stables. While the carpenter was calculating how much money he should ask to defray the cost of labour, wine, meat, bread and cheese for himself and his apprentices, the farmer launched into his litany for a second time.

"I have a great favour to ask of your lordship, being eager to sow my field with rye."

The Swedish cavalier interrupted his perambulations and paused in front of the man.

"You come here every year for bread and seed-corn," he said angrily. "You could feed yourself and your cow with your land and still save seed-corn enough to carry on your husbandry at a profit, but no! You sit drinking in the tavern from early morning onward, and when you're not in the tavern you're lying beside the stove at home. No wonder you never prosper! Thirst you know how to conquer, but when hunger threatens you come running to me."

The farmer knew that he had to ride out the storm before getting his half-bushel of seed-corn. He bowed his head and let the tirade flow over him, twisting his rabbitskin cap in his hands. After a while he began again:

"It being ancient custom that the lord of the manor should gladly and willingly hearken to his peasants' requests, greeting them in a friendly, earnest manner as befits a Christian gentleman, I have a great and important favour to ask of your lordship in respect of seed-corn. I only wish to borrow some."

"There goes another," said Maria Agneta, who, because the light was almost gone, had laid aside her book of engravings and walked to the window. "That's the third this week, God save us. Why do so many die there, and has my lord bishop no graveyard on his estate?"

"No," the schoolmaster told her. "He has naught but forges and smelting furnaces and numerous mines and galleries, St Matthew's Pit being the largest. Men are at liberty to die on his estate, but his bailiff sends them for burial to the villages round about."

Outside in the fading light a wretched funeral procession could be seen descending the hill to the highroad. A man bearing a cross came first, followed by an elderly priest. Then came a scrawny nag pulling the cart on which the wooden coffin reposed. There were no mourners in sight.

"I'm told," the carpenter volunteered, "that His Grace wishes to install a new pleasure-garden at his residence in Franconia, complete with pools and waterfalls, grottoes and fountains, Chinese pavilions and an orangery. That will cost money, but the diocesan coffers are empty. Accordingly, a new bailiff has been engaged. He has reduced the workers' rations. They now get no lard and only half a pound of bread a day, but they're compelled to work as hard as ever."

"Perhaps my lord bishop is ignorant of what goes on," said Maria Agneta. "Perhaps he should be told."

"He knows it only too well," the schoolmaster told her. "Folk hereabouts call him 'the Devil's Ambassador', and not without good reason. He has an imperious disposition – he wishes his household to surpass that of any secular prince in splendour. For his taste, no bailiff or pit-master could be hard enough on those poor souls."

The Swedish cavalier stood at the window, gazing in silence at the cart as it bore its burden slowly along the highroad with the old priest going on ahead.

"There's war on every side," the schoolmaster continued, "and that, to the diocesan estate, is a godsend. Charles of

Sweden and the Muscovite Tsar need an abundance of artillery, heavy and light, together with musket barrels, cuirasses and sword-blades. The bishop's chimneys belch smoke and his forges are aglow with red-hot iron. Heavy-laden waggons leave there for Poland every day."

"The diocesan estate is the last refuge of the doomed and the damned," the farmer said quietly from beside the door. "There's no escape – none but a merciful death."

All at once, carried away by the potency of his memories, the Swedish cavalier began to speak.

"Tending the limekilns," he said, "that's the worst work of all. Some are stone-breakers who loosen the rock with heavy crowbars and break it off with their bare hands, others smash it with iron mallets. They swallow dust, day after day, until, only a few years hence, they start to spit blood and waste away. God have mercy on them, likewise on those that are fettered to the carts that haul the crushed rock to the kilns and remove the burned lime. Each kiln has five glowing stokeholes . . ."

"But Christian," Maria Agneta said in astonishment, "how do you know all this? You speak as if you yourself had been a stone-breaker in the bishop's inferno."

"In the old days," he replied, "when I was riding courier on the highroad, I encountered many poor thieves and vagrants who told me of it." He paused for a moment before continuing. "In front of the kiln is the furnace, which has two blazing mouths, one to receive firewood, the other for the removal of red-hot ashes and embers. The furnace needs three to tend it: the fireman, the stoker, and the raker. The stoker has to heat the furnace by degrees. He feeds it first with shavings, then with bundles of brushwood, then with split logs which he scatters and distributes with his iron fork. The raker rakes the glowing debris from the furnace, so he has to be good at withstanding heat. Sometimes, however, when there's a wind blowing, the fiery breath of the furnace sears his face and hair, and his screams can be heard a long way off. The fireman regulates the fire. The flames are almost black with smoke at first, but then they change colour, becoming dark red, violet, blue, and, last of all, white. When the flames are white and the rock has turned a pretty pink, the firing is successful. The fireman must always keep his eye to the peephole, for if the fire fails to spread properly, let alone goes out, the batch is spoiled and the overseers thrash the fireman and his assistants with their whips. In winter, when the three men stream with sweat at their work in front of the glowing stokehole, and they step out into the icy air, Death comes to summon his victims. And when one of them is summoned and sinks to the ground with burning cheeks, every breath like a dagger-thrust in the ribs, all he gets for his pains is, 'Out of the way! If you're sick, lie down, draw your last breath, and die. Who needs you? No one!"

He fell silent. Maria Agneta lit the lamp. Maria Christine, who had fled the schoolmaster's primer and tiptoed off to play with her toys, could be heard urging her wooden horse along with jubilant little cries of "Gee-up!" Meanwhile, down on the highroad, the makeshift hearse was passing the manor house.

The Swedish cavalier bowed his head, and his lips moved in a silent prayer.

"Who's there, Papa?" Maria Christine inquired from her corner. "I can see you speaking, but I cannot hear you."

"I'm saying a Paternoster for a poor man's soul," he replied. "Who knows, he may have been some noble flower that withered and died before its time. Come and pray with me."

He picked up the child in his arms and returned to the window. Looking down at the highroad, Maria Christine caught sight of the horse-drawn cart. She laughed delightedly and broke into more cries of "Gee-up!"

"Enough of that," her father told her with a frown. "You're to say a Paternoster for a poor man's soul, didn't you hear?"

His voice had an unfamiliar, frightening ring. Close to tears, the little girl put her arms around his neck and repeated the words of the Lord's Prayer while the coffin-laden cart passed by in the dusk and disappeared from view.

★

131

At noon one day, when the carpenters had almost completed their work and the Swedish cavalier was crossing the farmyard with a caulking-iron in his hand, he saw two men standing in the gateway. His blood ran cold and his heart pounded madly, but he gave no sign of it and made to walk past them with an indifferent air, as if they were strangers to him. Six years had elapsed since their last meeting, he reflected, so it was possible that mere chance had brought them to Kleinroop, and that they would fail to recognise him. But no, they stepped forward and barred his path. Veiland whipped off his leather cap, and Wryneck, bowing and sweeping the ground with his hat, hailed him with a broad smile on his bearded face.

"God's thunder, Captain, you swagger along looking as high and mighty as if you were third in rank only to the Emperor himself. Don't you know your old comrades any more?"

"Mark how glad he is to see us," grumbled Veiland. "He couldn't be more so. I told you before we came: uninvited guests are like cabbage without lard — no one relishes them. I never expected you to hasten to the butcher and pick out the best joint of veal to roast in our honour, Captain. Grant us a night's lodging in your stable or root cellar and I'll be quite content."

"Not I," said Wryneck. "He used to be our captain, when all's said and done. Have we fallen into disfavour with him? Captain, I'll bide here with you, and if you've need of someone to bid you good morning every day and ask, 'Did your lordship sleep well?', let that be my allotted task. You won't find me neglectful."

The Swedish cavalier still said nothing, but order was slowly returning to the whirlwind of thoughts in his head. As he saw it, fate had delivered him into the hands of two erstwhile comrades who were now his mortal enemies. There was nothing he could do but steal away, renouncing house and home, wife and child, field and meadow, and hide himself in some foreign land, there to forget all that was dear to him. His fear and fury, torment and despair overflowed.

132

"You scoundrels!" he burst out in a choking voice. "Can't you leave me in peace? I thought the Devil had carried you off long since. What concern are you of mine?"

"Why so vehement, Captain?" Wryneck said reproachfully. "You call me a scoundrel, yet I've always been the best of comrades to you. I was sure you'd give us shelter in brotherly love and good faith. We've fallen on hard times, can't you see?"

"But I made you rich to the tune of many hundreds of thalers and ducats," the Swedish cavalier hissed. "Where are they?"

"They vanished down our gullets to no purpose," Wryneck told him.

"Man's three greatest afflictions, Captain," sighed Veiland, "are wenching, dicing, and drinking. I should have tossed a little of my money into running water, as the custom is. Covetous Satan would then have had his share, but now he has it all. The Devil sets up shop wherever there's a barrel and spigot."

"And when all was gone and we could keep the wolf from the door no longer," Wryneck added in conclusion, "we took to the road once more with staff and satchel."

The Swedish cavalier stared into space. He was breathing quickly, and an angry, menacing light shone in his eyes. He wouldn't go – no, he couldn't abandon the house and estate, he must stay and cling with both hands to all that he had wrested from heaven and earth. These two men here, Veiland and Wryneck, were obstacles to his continuing good fortune. If they came to grief, the fault would not be his – after all, who had asked them to come? He must silence them for ever, and at that thought he braced his arms and the caulking-iron grew heavy in his hand.

"Who showed you the way here?" he asked. "How did you know where to find me?"

"The Brabanter told us," Wryneck explained. "He's become a merchant at Ratibor – he trades in dyewoods and all manner of spices such as cinnamon, ginger, nutmegs, cloves and pepper. He has attained high office and sits in the council chamber – you should see how his fellow townsfolk respect him! The first time we came he welcomed us most heartily, sent his minions out of the room and closed the door behind them. We sat there drinking wine by the bottle and eating our fill of all there was, and when we departed he gave us each ten thalers to drink his health with. When next we called on him, however, we had to beg him on bended knee before he would toss us a guilder across the table with many a 'would if I had it'. Then came the third time. 'What, are you here again, you pests?' he bellowed. 'It's money, always money with you! Do you mean to bankrupt me? Go to our captain, who's become a nobleman and lives on his estate – he possesses all that a man could wish for.' And then he told us where you could be found."

"May the Devil reward him!" the Swedish cavalier hissed between clenched teeth. "And who told him I was here? I didn't shout it from the rooftops."

"He caught sight of you at the horse fair in Oppeln a year or eighteen months since," said Wryneck. "While sitting over a glass in the 'Golden Crown' he saw you strolling across the marketplace, arm in arm with sundry persons of quality. He knew you at once, so he took the landlord aside and asked him who you were and where you lived, and the landlord told him. He also said you breed the finest foals for many miles around."

The Swedish cavalier had made up his mind. The men in question had proved themselves good comrades and survived many dangers in his company, but fear and rage outweighed all else. They had wormed their way back into his life, so he must make them disappear for ever, these two first and then the Brabanter. His thoughts turned to a lonely spot not far from the manor house. It was there in the gully, where the stream flowed between clumps of willow, that the deed would be done.

"So now there are three that know who I was," he said, half to himself. "I must have a care, or there'll soon be a hundred."

"What the deuce are you saying?" cried Wryneck, who had caught the last few words. "I'll vouch for the Brabanter as I would for myself. Were all the headsmen in the Holy Roman Empire to come and cut his hide in ribbons for a wager, he would never betray you."

"That's true, I won't deny it," the Swedish cavalier replied with every appearance of relief and satisfaction. "Now listen: I have my money buried in a safe place not far from here, and I'll share it with you for old friendship's sake. Take a shovel each and come with me."

He pointed to some garden tools hanging on a nearby wall. Veiland, looking surprised and thoughtful, made no move to obey, but Wryneck hurled his hat in the air and shouted for joy.

"Hallelujah! Glory to be God! All our troubles are over, thank heaven! A long and happy life to you, Captain!"

The Swedish cavalier beckoned to them to take their shovels and follow him, but he turned to find himself confronted by Maria Christine, who had come up behind him unheard. She tugged at his sleeve.

"Papa," she piped in a tone of reproof, "why don't you come? Mother sent me – the dishes are on the table."

"Is this your lordship's little daughter?" Wryneck asked very deferentially, not wishing the child to see how closely acquainted he was with the lord of the manor.

"Yes," said the Swedish cavalier, "it is."

Maria Christine surveyed the two ragged figures for a while, quite undaunted, then plucked again at her father's sleeve.

"What men are these, Papa? Are they good men? I've never seen them before."

"They've come looking for work on the estate," he replied curtly.

Wryneck knelt down beside his former captain's daughter and engaged her in conversation.

"Little princess," he said, "your face is as pink and white as the loveliest of tulips. You can hop from foot to foot, so I see, but what else can you do?"

Maria Christine stood on a stone to make herself look taller.

"I can say the alphabet," she told him, "and I can dance the courante and sarabande and play the clavichord, though not very well – I've only just begun to learn it. What can you do?"

"I can do all manner of things," Wryneck declared. "I can shoe a goose and pick fleas off a hedgehog. I make coloured aprons for grasshoppers, and fish jump out of their ponds when I whistle."

Maria Christine stared at him with parted lips and eyes like saucers. Then she pointed to Veiland.

"And he, what can he do?"

"He can make short sausages out of long in a trice," Wryneck replied, laughing. "That's his best trick, but he can also bray like a donkey and hiss like a goose. What's more, he can imitate the sound of a cat and a dog fighting."

"I should like to hear a cat and dog fighting," said Maria Christine.

Veiland needed no second bidding. He began to purr, yap, hiss, growl, bark, howl, and snarl angrily, and when he was done and the dog ran off whimpering, Maria Christine clapped her hands and hopped from foot to foot in a transport of delight.

"You mustn't go, either of you – I won't have it. No cat or dog could do better. You must stay here on the estate, but remember: the workfolk eat at noon and six o'clock sharp, and anyone who isn't there betimes with his mug gets no ale."

Her father was astonished to see how promptly and trustfully she had taken to the two ragged fellows, and his heart grew lighter. Neither of the men who had shown off their foolish tricks for her benefit would ever betray him, he was sure of that now. He saw them for what they truly were: two poor comrades in adversity who had come, not to destroy his happiness, but because they hoped that they would fare better at his door than by begging a morsel of bread from a stranger. Banished by a child's laughter, the thought of murder receded from his mind.

"Because my little daughter has bidden you welcome," he said, "you may remain. All else apart, I think it better for you to be near me than far away. Now go to the farmhands' quarters and get yourselves a bowl of cabbage soup with bacon in it, and when you've eaten I'll see how best to employ the pair of you. There are sheep to be sheared and oats to be sown and stones to be culled from the fields, and the orchard will soon have need of a watchful eye. Meantime, God go with you, but bear one thing in mind: old tales are not worth the telling."

He walked off with Maria Christine skipping along beside him. His two new farmhands watched him until he disappeared into the house. Then Wryneck heaved a sigh.

"Did it strike you? He said not another word about the money or his offer to share it with us. Methinks our pitcher got broken on the way to the well. We weren't destined to fill it after all, and must remain poor."

Veiland, who could hear a horse whinny three hours' march away and a cock crow at two leagues, shook his head.

"I'd rather have it so," he said. "When he spoke of the money and bade us come with him, my legs refused to budge for some strange reason. From now on I shall spend my days bending and toiling and culling stones from the fields and supping off cabbage soup with bacon in it. I can't say why, God knows, but I'd rather it were so."

The two new farmhands were seldom seen together because Wryneck wielded dandy-brush and curry-comb in the stables while Veiland worked in the fields at ploughing, sowing, and harrowing. They remained friends, however, and spent every evening in the stables playing cards, drinking their measure of wine together, and generally seeing eye to eye. They had little to do with the other workfolk, but when Wryneck espied Maria Christine from afar he would whistle to her to come to him in the stables. The wooden chest he kept there always held some new surprise for her, whether it was a reed pipe or a monkey with movable limbs carved from a block of wood and painted in divers colours.

The Swedish cavalier they shunned as far as possible, for they no longer regarded him as their equal. To them he was now the noble lord of the manor, and they feared that he might one day regret having taken them into his service. Whenever he came to inspect the stables or they unwittingly happened to cross his path, they stood at attention like soldiers before their lieutenant. Neither their manner nor their speech betrayed that they shared a secret with him.

They persevered in this way of life until one night, a year later, the Swedish cavalier's fortunes were laid in ruins by a bolt from the blue.

He was entertaining some noblemen from the city that evening, and it was somewhat later than his wont when he got up from the table and asked his guests to excuse him while he conducted a rapid tour of inspection. He had left the house and was studying the weather when Wryneck accosted him. The man clearly had something to say but did not know how to begin, and the Swedish cavalier, being pressed for time, grew impatient.

"Well, what is it?" he snapped. "Haven't you eaten your fill?"

"Yes indeed, your lordship," said Wryneck. "We had millet gruel and red sausage at noon and, just now, beer soup and bread and cheese for supper. With all due respect, however, I came to apprise your lordship of another matter. Someone has expressed a humble desire to speak with your lordship. I not only know him, I know that your lordship is acquainted with him. He came post-haste – his carriage is waiting outside the gate – and I fear that his presence bodes no good."

"Who the devil is it?" the Swedish cavalier demanded. "Be brief, I've no time to waste."

"I didn't recognise the man – it was too dark," Wryneck replied, contradicting himself. "Your lordship will see for himself who it is."

The Swedish cavalier's voice sank to an angry whisper.

"Out with it, fellow! Is it the Bloody Baron?"

"No, as God's my witness," Wryneck whispered back. "May it please your lordship, its the Brabanter. I was afraid to say so, being forbidden to tell old tales because your lordship has no wish to hear them."

The Swedish cavalier turned away with an impatient gesture and made for the gateway. The Brabanter stepped out of the shadows into the lanternlight.

No one would have recognised him as the villain of yore. He looked like a man alive to his own importance and the universal esteem in which others held him. He wore silken hose, breeches of cherry-red velvet, and a black camisole richly embroidered with silver thread. A sword hung at his side and a lorgnette dangled from the gold chain around his neck. His movements were measured, and every word he spoke was imbued with quiet, imperturbable dignity.

"A very good evening to you," he began. "You can scarce believe your eyes, from the look of you. I doubt if you expected us to meet again."

"I always knew that you would not deprive me of your friendship," the Swedish cavalier rejoined in a faintly mocking tone. "Well, what news? What brings you here? Did you come to talk of bygone days?"

"No," said the Brabanter. "My visit is occasioned by present circumstances. But let me look at you, Captain! I rejoiced to hear that you had so nobly acquitted yourself in your present station. Everyone admires you and utters your name with respect. I say that because it's the truth, not for courtesy's sake."

"Many thanks," said the Swedish cavalier. "I'm honoured that you should take such a friendly interest in my doings. And you? How do you earn your living?"

"In trade," the Brabanter replied. "How would the mouse fare without its oaten straw? I've made my fortune by buying and selling at a modest profit. My capital remains untouched."

"And in other respects? How do you employ your time? Have you a wife and children?"

The Brabanter shook his head. "No. I could have had a physician's daughter but thought it more beneficial to remain unwed. In the evenings, when I've dispatched my correspondence, I go to the theatre or an assembly. There I converse with friends or sometimes, *pour passer le temps*, indulge in a hand of cards. On Sundays, whenever the weather is fine, I take my ease in the garden. That is how it has been hitherto. Now, however, I've converted all I own into money, even the furniture and paintings in my house, and am leaving the country."

"For myself," said the Swedish cavalier, "I think it likely that I shall grow old and grey here on my estate. The master must be stronger than his land, so they say, but it often turns out that the land proves stronger than its master – it clings to him and won't let him go. Being at liberty to visit foreign lands, unlike me, you're truly to be envied."

"Is anyone in the world to be envied?" the Brabanter replied. "When I reflect on the strange vicissitudes in my life, past and present, the futility and impermanence of worldly pleasures become all too plain. Everything passes, just as a candle goes out when its time is up. We're merely a ball in the hands of fickle Dame Fortune. The higher she tosses us into the air, the harder we fall."

"Your philosophising merits admiration," said the Swedish cavalier, "but it's of no use to me. I've no time for such things. I have to provide for my wife and child and the many workfolk on my estate."

The Brabanter did not speak for a moment. Then, in a low, urgent voice, he said, "Listen, Captain. It grieves me to have to tell you this, but I bring bad news. You must leave here."

"Why, what's up?" the Swedish cavalier demanded, as yet with no trace of alarm or concern in his voice.

"You must leave here," the Brabanter repeated. "Go at once. The Bloody Baron is after you."

The Swedish cavalier shrugged.

"The Bloody Baron?" he said with a curt laugh. "If that's all it is . . . Let him come, I don't care. What does he know of me?"

"Of the master of Kleinroop not much," the Brabanter replied, "but he knows all about the Desecrators and their captain, for Red Lisa has turned traitor. That's why I urge you to leave at once."

Just then, Maria Agneta's voice rang out across the darkened courtyard.

"Christian, where are you? We've been waiting so long. Your guests are grumbling at you for deserting them in favour of the stables."

She had opened a window and was leaning out. A hubbub of laughing, disputing voices issued from the room behind her.

"I'm coming, dearest," the Swedish cavalier called, "be patient a little while longer." He turned back to the Brabanter. "You spoke of Red Lisa. What of her?"

"Is that Madame de Tornefeld?" the Brabanter inquired, peering through his lorgnette.

"Yes, that's my wife. She's the best, the purest, most saintly woman alive, and what am I?"

"*Sublime, adorable!*" the Brabanter murmured, pursing his lips admiringly as Maria Agneta left the window and disappeared from view. "You should commission a portrait of her in oils, gouache or tempera," he added. "Please convey my apologies for failing to present *mes hommages.*"

"What of Red Lisa?" the Swedish cavalier insisted. "Quickly, you heard her call me."

"Our luck is out, Captain," the Brabanter told him. "Red Lisa took up with a corporal in the Bloody Baron's dragoons, who are quartered at Schweidnitz, and married him. It wasn't long before her love for you turned to hatred. The corporal is a youngster, and she wishes him to gain promotion, so she sent a message to the Bloody Baron –"

"Where is he?" the Swedish cavalier broke in. "Is he still a captain of dragoons?"

"He was in Spain and Hungary, and latterly on official business in Vienna, but now I'm told he's on the way to Schweidnitz. He's a colonel now, and Red Lisa boasts that she'll deliver us into his hands. Her corporal has already been promised an officer's commission, she says, and we can count ourselves lucky if we're branded on the forehead and sent to serve His Majesty in the galleys. Put your affairs in order and begone, Captain. You've everything to fear from her thirst for revenge."

The Swedish cavalier knit his brow and stared up at the lantern over the gateway.

"The matter's bad enough," he said at length, "but it could be worse. Why should I go? I'd do better to remain where I am. Red Lisa knows nothing about me. She'll go looking for me on the highroad, in taverns, at markets and fairs – wherever humble folk congregate – but not on a manorial estate."

"Captain," said the Brabanter, "you surprise me greatly. You speak as if you'd banished your five senses to the East Indies. Red Lisa knows very well where to look for you. Didn't you often let slip that you aspired to become a nobleman? Once, when you lay sick with the fever and she was bathing your face with vinegar-water, you upbraided the workfolk you saw in your dreams, calling them an idle, shiftless, thieving crew and warning them that you would rule them with a rod of iron when you returned to the estate a year hence. Such were the thoughts that exercised your mind. On the day we parted, Red Lisa told me that anyone wishing to find you would only have to go the rounds of the manor houses. That's why I urge you to –"

"How can she hope to find me?" the Swedish cavalier interposed, but a note of uncertainty had crept into his voice. "There are many hundreds of manor houses in Pomerania, Poland, Brandenburg and elsewhere."

"She'll not have far to seek," the Brabanter replied. "The Bloody Baron need only make inquiries and he'll soon discover that you came here seven or eight years ago with your saddlebags full of money. Once his suspicions have fastened upon you and he confronts you with Red Lisa so that she can testify against you, what then? Waste no time – do as I am doing. I'd rather be content with a pittance than live in constant danger. Take my advice and get away from here, Captain. People dwell beyond the mountains too, you know."

"Yes," the Swedish cavalier said quietly, "I should go, I suppose, but my heart won't let me."

"Stay, then, and get yourself branded and hanged!" the Brabanter burst out. "Why did I trouble to speak at all? There's none so deaf as won't hear."

He took a watch from his fob, a repeater of enamelled gold, and held it to his ear.

"I must go, my coachman awaits me," he went on more calmly. "Why should I vex myself? It's your neck that's at stake, not mine. I've told you all, so you've been warned. If you come to grief, it'll be no fault of mine."

They walked in silence down the avenue of maples to the Brabanter's carriage. The coachman saluted and climbed on the box. The Brabanter got in. Leaning out of the window, he spoke in a voice too low to be overheard.

"I respect your courage, Captain. You mean to stay ·and weather the storm, but I'm sorry for your daughter's sake. She'll have to live out her life in the knowledge that her father was branded on the forehead with the wheel and gibbet and sent in chains to the galleys. And now, Captain, fare you well. *Allons!* Coachman, drive on!"

The Swedish cavalier stood watching the carriage as it receded into the darkness. The Brabanter's words had pierced him to the heart like a stiletto. He knew now that he must go – he must go for his child's sake, but where to?

And then, as he stood there listening to the sound of wheels fading in the distance, he had a momentary vision.

He saw himself mounted on his dun charger in his blue Swedish tunic, one cavalryman among many. They were riding across a vast expanse of open heath with carrion crows circling in the sky above, which was heavily overcast. All around him voices were singing the Swedish anthem, cannon thundering, torn banners fluttering, musket balls thudding into the serried ranks. One of them struck him, and with an inexpressible feeling of contentment, he slid from his horse to the ground.

That night he told Veiland and Wryneck what he had learned from the Brabanter and bade them hold themselves in readiness to accompany him to the Swedish war. They greeted the news with delight and drank a toast to their captain's health, for they had long since grown weary of working on the estate and welcomed any change in their way of life. Eager for a return to the good old days when they had roamed the countryside like hawks in search of prey, they hoped that the war would enable them to replenish their pockets with loot under their captain's command.

It was a sad moment for the Swedish cavalier and an even sadder one for Maria Agneta when he told her that he must join the King of Sweden in the Ukrainian steppe for service against the Muscovites. She stared at him, uncertain if she had heard him aright, and he was obliged to tell her a second time: like other Swedes residing abroad, he had last night received express orders from the King's headquarters to join the Swedish army forthwith, escorted by two well-mounted servants

She burst into tears. Racked with sobs, she accused him of thinking only of martial glory and of his king, who meant everything to him, whereas she herself counted for nothing. His love for her was dead, she declared.

He disputed this, but he could not tell her the truth: that concern for her and their child's good name and future happiness had compelled him to sever his destiny from theirs, and that, far from seeking martial glory in the Swedish army, he hoped to find the honourable death that would be denied him if he remained at home.

"My dearest darling," he told her time and again, "you know that my love for you is anything but dead. It burns within me constantly. You're my good angel and my joy, and nothing will ever make me profess otherwise, but go I must. For seven years I've stood idly by. Now my king has issued the summons for which I had always to be prepared. Don't weep, dearest. Didn't you promise me, in love and good faith, to accept good and ill alike at my hands?"

"And you?" she said despairingly, holding him close. "Didn't you swear to abide with me till death do us part? How shall I endure the time without you, and what do I care for your king, to whom glory has always meant more than any woman alive?"

"Do not speak so of His Majesty's noble person," he told her. "I yearn to stay, my dearest, but it cannot be. The time has come for me to buckle on my sword. I leave you with a heavy heart, God knows, but my king has summoned me."

She wept all that day and throughout the night that followed. In the morning a benumbed serenity came over her. She went to the closet and took out the blue Swedish tunic with the brass buttons and red collar, the elk-leather breeches, the yellow gauntlets, the sword with the leather hilt, the feed bag, canteen, and cavalry pistols. And when she saw them all arrayed there, she was assailed by a vision of the day when the Swedish cavalier had come to meet her in the sunlit garden with his hat beneath his arm.

"May God in His mercy preserve both you and your king," she said softly, stroking the threadbare blue tunic, and her eyes filled with tears.

Maria Christine came skipping into the stable to find Wryneck seated on his wooden chest in the gloom, mending an old saddle-girth. She watched him at his work for a while before broaching the subject that filled her with such alarm and curiosity.

"My father's off to the war, did you know?"

"Yes," said Wryneck, "and I and my comrade are riding with him."

"That makes three of you," she said, counting on her fingers. "Why are all three of you going, like the Three Wise Kings?"

"So that, when two say nothing, there'll be a third to listen to them."

"Is it far to the war?" she asked.

"Give me a yardstick and I'll measure it out," he told her.

"And when will you return?"

"When you've worn out three little pairs of shoes, that's when."

"But I want to know the day of your return," she insisted.

"Run into the woods and ask the cuckoo," Wryneck advised her. "He'll tell you the day."

"What will you do in the war?" she asked.

"I'll line my pockets," he replied. "My empty purse is a burden to me. I carry it more easily when it's full."

"Mother's weeping," she said. "Many men go to war and never return, she says."

"That shows you war's a good thing," Wryneck argued. "If it were a bad one, they'd all return in a trice."

"Why is Mother weeping, then?"

"Because she can't ride with us."

"Why can't she?"

"On account of the weather. What would she do at the war when it rains and snows?"

Maria Christine stamped her foot. "But I don't want my father to be at the war when it rains and snows. He's put on his old blue jacket, and it'll be wet through in a minute. He must return home before the bad weather comes."

"Don't be angry," Wryneck told her. "I'll see what I can do about it."

"You must help me," she said, clambering on his knee. "I know you can. I won't have my father staying away at the war, do you hear? Don't pretend to be deaf! You know all manner of tricks. Make him come home again."

"You behave as if my only duty is to do your bidding," Wryneck said, laughing. "You could wheedle a lost soul out of the Devil himself. Leave my beard alone, you'll pluck it out by the roots. Now listen: if you truly wish your father to come back from the war, take some salt and some earth and put them in a little bag."

"Salt and earth," she repeated. "What kind of earth? Black earth, red earth?"

"Earth is earth, be it red or yellow, black or brown. Put the salt and earth in a little bag and stitch it into your father's blue tunic between the cloth and the lining. But you must do it by moonlight, and no one must see you with the needle and thread in your hand, nor must any dog bark nor any cock crow, or the spell will be broken and you must start all over again. Do you understand?"

"Yes," she whispered.

"Salt and earth concealed in a garment," Wryneck pursued, "are so potent a spell that he'll think of you day and night. They're stronger than any bell-rope – they'll bind him to you so tightly that he'll never rest, day or night, until he's back with you once more. Can you remember all that?"

"Yes," she said in a tremulous voice, for her heart quailed at the thought that the spell must be cast at dead of night. "Fill a little bag with salt and earth and then, with needle and thread –"

"By moonlight, mark you, not candlelight," Wryneck warned her. "Don't forget that. The moon was new eleven days ago – it's still waxing. Now could be the time."

That night, when the moon had risen above the copper beeches and alder bushes in the garden, Maria Christine slipped out of bed. From under her pillow she took the sachet of salt and soil, a small pair of scissors, and a needle and thread. Then she stole out of her bedchamber and tiptoed silently upstairs. Another few steps, a brief pause outside the door to reassure herself that all was quiet, and she made her way, with a pounding heart, into the room where her father's blue tunic lay draped over an armchair.

The big room was not entirely in darkness. Moonlight streamed through the window, picking out various objects. The brass buttons on the blue Swedish tunic gleamed faintly. Maria Christine took a step forward and gave a little start at the sight of her reflection moving in the mirror on the wall. As soon as she grasped that she was alone in the room, she drew a deep breath and took the tunic from the chair. It was surprisingly heavy. Clasping it to her, she half-carried, half-dragged it to the window and crouched down beside it with bated breath, fearful lest some dog might bark or cockerel crow and render all her surreptitious labours in vain. But the dogs and cockerels held their peace, so she spread the tunic across her lap and picked up the scissors.

Although the dogs and cockerels were asleep at this hour, her mother and father were still awake. Maria Agneta was sitting in the Long Room, her face pale and tear-stained, while her husband stood in front of the fireplace with folded arms.

As he gazed into the dying embers, his thoughts returned to the moment when he had first set eyes on Maria Agneta, here in this very room. It was here that she had stood, a poor girl duped by all around her, complaining that her sweetheart had forgotten her and their love. It was here, too, that he, the Bloody Baron's helpless captive, had first been smitten with the presumptuous idea that she must become his wife, and that he would make a better nobleman than the youth in question, both in her eyes and in those of the world at large. What others were born with, he had been compelled to fight for and procure by devious, daring, illicit means. There now remained but one last thing for him to do: having been granted seven years of life as a nobleman, he was duty-bound to die like one. That death he had resolved to seek in the Swedish army, and he was grateful to Providence for sparing him an ignominious end on the gallows.

"Our workfolk are good, honest, skilful souls," he told Maria Agneta. "You need only husband your resources and you'll want for nothing."

"Nothing save you, my dearest," she said in a low voice, "but that you give no thought to."

"You must also ensure," he went on, "that the household, stables and fields are thriftily administered without in any way being neglected. Never spend more than the estate brings in. Get rid of useless livestock without delay. Don't be overhasty with the summer sowing – it's better to wait for fine weather. And never forget: one field well ploughed and manured yields more than two in poor condition."

"How am I to think of all that," she said plaintively, "when

148

I shall be living in constant dread? My heart will be eaten away with fear."

But his thoughts had already turned to his flock of sheep, which had made him a tidy profit. He was just explaining to Maria Agneta that good grass alone produced good wool and advising her on how to protect the flock against scours and scabies when he stopped short, startled by a sound that seemed to come from the adjoining room. He put a finger to his lips.

"What was that?" he said. "Did you hear it? Who in the house would still be awake at this hour?"

"No one," Maria Agneta replied. "A gust of wind must have caught one of the shutters."

But he thought he heard floorboards creaking underfoot. Taking the candlestick from the table, he went to the door and flung it open.

"Hey!" he called. "Who's there?"

The little girl's heart had thumped at every stitch, for she could hear her father's voice quite close at hand. She had completed her work at last without interference from dog or cockerel, and was thankfully draping the blue tunic over the armchair once more, when something heavy tumbled to the floor beside her.

Maria Christine flinched at this inexplicable noise and made quickly for the door, only to collide with a chair. She grimaced with pain, close to tears, and rubbed her hip and knee before hurrying on. She lost a slipper in her haste and paused, wondering what to do for the best. Then she found the missing slipper, stepped into it, and darted out of the room just as her father called "Who's there?"

Man and wife stood in the doorway for a few moments, he with the candlestick raised, she nestling anxiously against him. All at once, as he moved his arm, the candlelight fell on the copper-bound cover of a book lying on the floor beside the armchair. Maria Agneta hurried over and picked it up.

"That was it," she said. "That was what made such a noise as it fell. The cat must have tried to pull your coat off the chair

149

and the book slipped out of the pocket. It looks a hundred years old – it smells of mildew."

The Swedish cavalier had forgotten all about Tornefeld's arcanum during his years of prosperity. He regarded it thoughtfully.

"It's a bible that belonged to Gustavus Adolphus, the celebrated hero," he told her. "He had it beneath his corselet when death laid him low. I was instructed to deliver it into the young king's own hands, but I doubt if it'll bring me much honour, it's in so sorry a state, with its stained, worm-eaten pages. I fear His Majesty will set little store by such trash."

He shrugged, but took the book notwithstanding and tossed it on to the table beside his cavalry pistols and yellow gauntlets.

At dawn two days later, when the fish-pond and meadows were still wreathed in mist, the Swedish cavalier rode out of the courtyard with Veiland and Wryneck. His leavetaking had been a sad and painful one, and when Maria Agneta embraced him for the last time and commended him to Christ's all-powerful protection with quivering lips and tremulous voice, it was all he could do not to tell her that they were parting for ever.

The little girl, who was still asleep, did not wake when he kissed her lightly on the lips, brow, and eyelids.

PART FOUR

The Nameless Man

THE HOUR WAS LATE, and the Swedish cavalier was sitting over a half-empty mug of beer in the dank tap-room of a Polish inn. Though fatigued by his three days' ride through forest and marsh, he felt no desire to sleep. The landlord's dog lay stretched out on the flagstones, twitching as it dreamed of chasing hares, foxes, and wild boar. The landlord himself, who spoke only Polish, sat drinking with Veiland and Wryneck in a corner. He was on tenterhooks because his wife had gone into labour, and the other two were advising him on what to do for her. He should give her honey-water and pounded myrrh to drink, they told him, but he couldn't understand them and kept asking what they wanted.

The lamp was burning low. When silence fell in the tap-room, the woman's moans could be heard above the wind that whistled and rustled and whispered among the branches of the trees surrounding the inn.

Veiland and Wryneck drained their glasses of brandy and left the tap-room preceded by the landlord carrying a candle. The wooden stairs creaked under their tread. The Swedish cavalier sat motionless with his head bowed, for ever thinking of the estate he had left behind. Now that all was still, the familiar sounds and voices that had rung in his ears throughout the day returned to haunt him. For moments on end he heard disjointed snatches of the gossip exchanged by his peasant-women as they sat rippling flax of an evening; the creak of the courtyard gate; the draw-well's plaintive groan; the cooing of doves as Maria Agneta coaxed them back to the dovecote; the hiss of the grindstone; the bellow of an ox being harnessed to a waggon; the clatter of clogs and milk pails; his overseer

153

predicting a storm in the night; and, ever and again, the piping voice of Maria Christine calling piteously for her father and refusing to believe that he had ridden off.

He sat up abruptly, took Gustavus Adolphus' bible from his pocket, and tossed it on the table in front of him.

"You've undergone a wondrous transformation," he told it. "Once upon a time you egged me on from one escapade, one adventure, to the next. You bedazzled me day and night with the fortunes in gold and silver that lay strewn about the countryside and encouraged me to hunt them down. You showed me all that was there for the taking, but now, hour after hour, you blight my eyes with visions of all that I've lost for ever. Leave me in peace, I tell you. Stop tormenting me or, as true as there's a God above, I'll hurl you into the fire. I've had enough of you."

He fell silent, staring into space. Then he ran his hand over the old book's copper-bound cover.

"You may be right," he said, as if the dead king's bible had answered him. "How could I ever, from one day to the next, forget the sound of my dearest wife's voice and my daughter's joyous laughter, her singing and weeping? And why should I go to the war? You speak the truth. My hand is better suited to a peasant's spade then a soldier's musket. What would I do in the Swedish army? Burn villages, destroy peasants' grain and drive off their cattle, go foraging in farmhouses, frighten poor folk to death, harass them with oaths and curses: 'Bring out all you possess, you scum!' I'd be a fool to play the soldier for Charles of Sweden's sake, what with digging trenches, charging the enemy, and riding my horse into the ground. If Charles has a quarrel with the Tsar of Muscovy, that's his affair. He can live with him in peace or enmity, as he pleases. What do I care?"

The wind whistled, the dog barked in its sleep. The Swedish cavalier stared fixedly at the book in front of him.

"I've played a man's game, you know that," he said softly. "Am I to give it up for lost because of a wench that cannot forget?"

He thought of Red Lisa and how she had once truly, whole-heartedly loved him. She had been as devoted to him as any dog obedient to the very look in its master's eye. Could he not contrive to rekindle the embers of the love she had borne him? The longer he debated this question, the more hopeful he became of mastering his destiny once more. The game, so it seemed to him now, could still be won.

"I must make the attempt, there's no other way," he told himself. "If I succeed, I can return to my estate and these few days of misery will be no more than a bad dream. If not, the executioner may put an end to a nameless man."

Footsteps could be heard. The stairs creaked, the door opened, and Veiland and Wryneck appeared. He swiftly replaced the arcanum in his pocket.

"Why roam about so?" he demanded angrily. "Get some sleep while there's still time. We ride before daybreak."

"Are you really so eager to depart, Captain?" Wryneck asked. "There's a new Christian soul in the house, didn't you hear him bawling? A boy child, and the landlord, in his delight, has offered to ply us with food and drink for two whole days. Why shouldn't we take our ease? We'll get to the war in good time – it'll not run away from us."

"We're not going to the war," the Swedish cavalier told him. "I've changed my mind. We'll turn back and ride to Schweidnitz, where the dragoons are quartered, but my business is not with them. I've a matter of life and death to discuss with Red Lisa."

Wryneck stood there for a moment, transfixed with amazement, but he soon had some advice to hand.

"If you speak with her, Captain, fork out a thaler or two. Red Lisa always did think poverty the worst of vices. Spend a little money to prevent the worst from happening and you'll get off cheaply."

"To hell with that!" cried Veiland. "Listen to me, Captain: no long speeches, a stone about her neck, and into the river with her, that's my advice."

"Enough said," the Swedish cavalier told him firmly. "I'll

155

shut her mouth one way or another, even if my blood bespatters the headsman's axe in consequence. This is my last chance, and I mean to take it. I'm staking my life on this throw.''

"You're not dicing for hazelnuts, Captain, I know,'' said Wryneck, "but I'm not afraid on your account. You always were a daredevil. In days gone by, running the gauntlet 'twixt life and death was your favourite pastime.''

Hidden among bushes on the river bank an hour's ride from Schweidnitz stood a day-labourers' hut that had remained unoccupied for years. Here the three men bivouacked. They also found a barn in which to stable their horses, and at nightfall Veiland set off for the town to discover where Red Lisa and her corporal were lodging and when best to confront her.

"You've always been an excellent scout,'' the Swedish cavalier said as he sent him on his way, "so your part in this affair is paramount. Beware of letting her see your face, though – she would recognise you at once. You may have shaved your cheeks and chin, but you mustn't think you're greatly changed in appearance. Demonstrate your skill by all means, but do so with caution. Everything depends on you.''

"Let him go and rest easy,'' said Wryneck. "Knowing Veiland as I do, I also know there isn't a tree in all Silesia he'd care to hang from.''

Veiland was gone all that night, the following day, and the night thereafter. He returned having gleaned everything the Swedish cavalier required to know.

'The dragoons have been in Schweidnitz for some weeks now, purchasing remounts,'' he reported, "and Red Lisa and her corporal are lodging with a tailor in the lower part of the town – you need only ask for the house 'at the sign of the Green Tree'. The best time is the hour before midnight, when Red Lisa is alone in her chamber and the corporal sits in the tap-room of the 'Raven', drinking deep enough to turn a mill-wheel. At midnight, when he's well and truly drunk, he comes blundering upstairs and they start quarrelling fit to be heard from one end of the street to the other. The neighbours, being accustomed to this din, no longer heed it. I've also contrived a way for you to enter the house unobserved. At the point where it abuts on the courtyard and garden, there's firewood stacked against the wall. If you fetch the ladder from the garden shed and lean it against the woodpile –"

The Swedish cavalier cut him short. "How I get in is my business. Have you anything further to report?"

"Only that you owe me twenty-two kreuzers and a half for my food and two jugs of ale," said Veiland. "Tavern fare is mighty dear."

Late that afternoon the Swedish cavalier rode off to Schweidnitz escorted by Veiland. Wryneck remained behind in the hut with the pack-horse and valises, for he was known to several of the townsfolk and could not afford to show his face. When the other two reached the town they inquired the way to the best inn and turned in there. Rather than eat downstairs in the dining-room, the Swedish cavalier ordered an evening meal to be brought to his room. He had ridden far and was weary, he said, and his servant would wait on him at table.

The two men lurked unseen in their quarters until ten o'clock, when they slipped out of the inn and made for the lower part of town. Veiland led the way along sundry lanes and alleys to the courtyard adjoining the house "at the sign of the Green Tree".

"The tailor's still about – he's sitting in his workshop," he whispered, "but Red Lisa's room is in darkness. She can't be home yet."

"Unless she's abed," the Swedish cavalier whispered back, "having blown out the light and gone to sleep."

"No," came Veiland's whispered response, "she never goes to bed before her corporal returns."

The moon had disappeared behind a bank of cloud. The Swedish cavalier produced a bull's-eye lantern from beneath his cloak and shone it on the wall of the house – for a moment only, but long enough to gauge the distance between the window and the top of the woodpile and satisfy himself that he could reach it without the aid of a ladder. He also perceived how to open the shutters with little noise.

"Take this, I've no more need of it," he said, handing the lantern to Veiland. "And now, hurry back to the inn. Pay the landlord, fetch the horses from the stable, and station yourself nearby. Imitate the call of a goshawk or a buzzard so that I know when you're back and where to find you."

"Have you primed your pistols, Captain?" Veiland asked.

"Yes. Now hurry, in the name of a thousand devils!" commanded the Swedish cavalier, and he began to scale the wood-pile as Veiland disappeared into the darkness.

Red Lisa came in and closed the door behind her, slipping off her heavy shoes as she did so. The fire that smouldered on the hearth cast a faint glow over the floor. She took a few steps toward it and deposited a basket of eggs on the table in passing. Then, just as she was about to open the window, the room being smoky, she abruptly raised her head and listened: it seemed to her that she had caught the sound of someone breathing.

"Is that you, Jakob?" she called.

There was no answer. She could hear nothing, yet something told her that she was not alone in the room.

"Who's there?" she called in a hesitant voice.

Still no answer. She groped for a piece of kindling and thrust it into the embers. It flared up to reveal the figure of a man sitting motionless on her bed. Although she saw at once that it was not her Jakob, she was simply curious, not alarmed.

"Let's see what the wind's blown into my room," she said, and lit the stranger's face.

She uttered a low cry and staggered back in a shower of whirling sparks. An icy shiver ran down her spine. The hand holding the makeshift torch began to shake convulsively, the other hand clutched in vain at the air for support. The Swedish cavalier continued to sit motionless on the bed, gazing at Red Lisa from under his bushy eyebrows with a bold, mocking smile on his lips. His shadow danced wildly up and down on the wall behind him.

The piece of kindling fell to the floor and went out. Confused, disjointed thoughts raced through Red Lisa's mind.

Was it really the Captain? Was it possible? How long was it since she'd seen him? Did he know that she'd . . . Who could have told him? He'd looked at her with murder in his eyes. She ought to raise the alarm, call for help, but who would hear? The tailor had gout, and before the neighbours awoke . . . How he'd looked at her! Yes, that was how she'd remembered him all these years. What should she do, God help her? If Jakob . . . But Jakob wouldn't hear her. By the time he came at midnight it would be too late, she would be . . . The Captain would have . . . Jesus, who would come to her aid? He would make off through the window and disappear – no one was more elusive than the Captain – but he mustn't get away. She had him and must keep him there. No more need to go looking for him, and tomorrow, when the Bloody Baron . . . "We have him, Your Excellency!" All that money . . . She would never be poor again. He mustn't get away, even if she had to . . . Oh, Jesus, all that money . . .

"Why do you leave me sitting in the dark?" she heard her erstwhile captain say. "Strike a light!" She fetched a brand from the hearth and lit the tallow candle in the earthenware candlestick on the table, and while she did so she managed to set her thoughts in order. Having seen the pistol in his hand and the look of anger in his eyes, the look familiar to her from bygone days, she knew why he had come: her life was at stake. But she behaved as if she had nothing to fear from him – as if he were still a good companion whom she was overjoyed to see again after so many years. She began to speak, piling word on word to gain time. Meanwhile, she racked her brains for some way of saving her life and delivering her former lover into the Bloody Baron's clutches.

"So it's really you," she said, her tone conveying that she would never have dared to hope for so great a stroke of good fortune. "My hand is trembling, I can't think why. It must be my joy at seeing you again. How can I repay you for sparing the time to visit me? How did you get in, through the window? Still up to your old tricks, eh? You'll ruin my reputation with the neighbours. The next time you come, be sure to enter by the door – I'm a respectable housewife these days. Well, just look about you. Do you find my home comfortable?"

"Exceedingly so," he replied. Looking at her, he detected a callous, cunning expression that was new to him. It was clear that he had nothing to hope for from her love, which had long since faded and died. Red Lisa stood between him and his happiness, so she must be silenced for ever. He continued to hold the pistol steady, awaiting Veiland's signal.

"What of you?" she went on. "How have the years treated you? You haven't prospered unduly, from the look of you. Well, not everything has gone as I myself would have wished, but what matter? When I was troubled and afflicted with sleepless nights, I sought refuge in the bottle. Now, however, I've no more need of such consolation. Have you come to see how I'm faring in my new married state, Captain? If so, tell me by what name and title to present you to my Jakob, who'll be here before long. I'm for ever fancying that I hear his step on the stairs."

"Let him come," said the Swedish cavalier. "I'll send him back down the stairs and into hell."

"Goodness, what are you saying?" she exclaimed. "Can you really be so jealous as to have designs on my Jakob's life?"

Just then it came to her, quite suddenly, what she must do to ensure that her erstwhile lover fell into the Bloody Baron's hands. The plan that had taken shape in her mind was a terrible one, and she shrank from putting it into effect, deterred by a vestige of her former love. So tight were the iron bands around her heart that she almost cried out in fear and distress, but the moment soon passed. The hatred within her was stronger than all else. Had she not entreated God on her knees, time and again, to deliver this man into her hands so that she could repay him for what he had done to her? Well, now the moment had

160

come: he was at her mercy. She looked about her. Jakob's bag of tools lay beside the hearth, and the embers still glowed red. Her mind was made up, and her voice, as she continued to speak, betrayed no sign of what had taken place within her.

"Are you truly jealous?" She laughed. "You should have paid me greater regard instead of leaving me alone for so many years. Now it's too late. Take my advice: resign yourself. Don't pick a quarrel with my Jakob, he's very quick-tempered. You could be friends, after all. But now it's time for me to prepare his supper. The fire's going out, and I'll rue it if he returns to find no food on the table."

She took some eggs from the basket and broke them into a frying pan. Then she bent over the bag of tools and removed the iron with which regimental chargers were customarily branded on the left side of the neck. The regiment took its mark from the name of its colonel, Baron von Lilgenau, alias the Bloody Baron: it was an inch-high "L" which, when inverted, resembled a gibbet. Red Lisa thrust the iron into the fire as though stirring the embers into new life.

"He's very particular in that respect," she said as she straightened up, leaving the iron in the fire. "If his supper isn't ready betimes he grows quarrelsome. I've no other cause for complaint. He won't hear of my having a child – children would benefit neither of us, he says – but who knows? When he gains his promotion, and he's very well-liked by the officers of the regiment . . ."

Outside in the garden, the cry of a goshawk pierced the night. The Swedish cavalier rose and went over to her.

"Enough!" he said in a low but commanding voice. "Say a Paternoster – pray to Jesus and confess your sins. Your time is nearly up."

"Why should I say a Paternoster? What do you mean to do with me?" She fell back a step. "Have you taken up your old trade again? If you mean to ply it here, save yourself the trouble. I've no money in the house."

"I'm not after your money. You know very well why I came – you knew it from the first. Aren't you in league with the Bloody Baron? Didn't you offer to deliver me into his hands if he granted your husband an officer's commission?"

She brushed the hair out of her eyes and shrugged.

"So that's the way the wind blows," she said. "Who fed you such an arrant lie?"

Without waiting for an answer, she knelt beside the hearth and proceeded to poke the fire as if the omelette were her sole concern.

"You've nothing to fear from me," she went on, gripping the iron tightly. "I've always kept mum and shall continue to do so. I call heaven and earth to witness that I mean you no harm."

She heard a faint sound: the creak of the front door opening and closing. Her Jakob was home at last. She must do it now, before he entered the room – before his step was heard on the stairs. "Strike!" the voice within her whispered. "He's your enemy – yours and all mankind's, so strike without mercy!"

"Only a fool would believe that," she heard him say. "Stand up! Can you swear it by the cross that was made on your brow at baptism?"

She was on her feet in a flash. They stood facing each other for a fraction of a second. Then she thrust the red-hot iron at his forehead.

He gave a muffled cry and reeled backwards, clutching his brow, his face and body contorted with pain.

A moment later he regained his self-control. Slowly he straightened up, gritting his teeth to stifle an involuntary groan, and slowly, inch by inch, he raised the hand that held the pistol.

She had planned to blow out the candle when the deed was done and make for the door under cover of darkness, but now she stood rooted to the spot by the terrible look on her enemy's face. Her limbs refused to obey her, but not her voice. Jakob's footsteps could be heard approaching the door – she must warn him.

"Have a care, the Desecrator!" she screamed, and her voice was filled with terror and triumph, mortal fear and wild exultation. "Don't come in! I've burned the gibbet into his brow! Run as fast as you can, raise the alarm! I've branded him with the . . ."

The pistol roared. Red Lisa fell forward on her face, silenced for ever.

He had climbed down again and was leaning unsteadily against the woodpile when Veiland appeared out of the darkness.

"Here I am – over here!" Veiland hissed. "What happened? What was that I heard her shout about gibbets and branding? I was afraid for you."

"Away, away!" groaned the Swedish cavalier. Veiland seized him by the arm, led him to where the horses were tethered, and helped him into the saddle.

Wryneck sprang to his feet when they entered the hut. He stared in horror at his master's face.

"Holy Mother of God!" he cried. "What have they done to you? It's enough to frighten a Turk."

"Give me a drink," groaned the Swedish cavalier. "They're after me. I can never show my face again – I'll have to hide myself away like a frightened beast."

Wryneck handed him the pitcher, which he drained.

"I'm to blame," said Veiland. "I shouldn't have left him alone with her."

"What's to be done, Captain?" Wryneck cried. "Where to now?"

"Where to indeed," the Swedish cavalier muttered, his teeth chattering. "To the Devil's Ambassador, that's where! Into the spitting, crackling flames of the bishop's inferno – that's where I must go, now that I've been denied an honourable place in which to live and die."

The man known in the bishop's smeltery as "Poker" because of his unrivalled skill at tending the furnaces with a heavy iron rod – this Poker, a tall, broad-shouldered young fellow with cheeks scarred by fire and muscles as hard as rock, was making his way up the forest track that led from the bishop's domain to the outside world. He walked with slow, hesitant steps as though unused to going where he pleased. Nine long years he had spent as one of the living dead that served the bishop and tended his furnaces, and nine different tasks had been allotted him in that time. He had been a human draught-horse harnessed to a cart, a stone-breaker, a furnaceman, a stoker, a porter, a smelter, a foundryman, a coal-master, and, last of all, a kiln-master. As a kiln-master he had been spared continual thrashings from the bishop's foremen, and now he was free at last. Incredible though he found it, his servitude was at an end and the wide world lay before him with all its highways and byways, straight and crooked.

On he strode, heedless of the wind that pierced the rents and holes in his coarse smock. Whenever the fancy took him he reached in his pocket and jingled the money which the clerk in the bailiff's office had counted out on the desk the day before. Six guilders and a half – that was the extent of Poker's worldly wealth, and now he would see how far it took him. His foremost desire was to extricate himself from the forest. Reaching a fork in the track, he paused irresolutely, wondering whether to turn right or left – to take the bellows or the windward side, as his luckless comrades in the smeltery would have termed it.

"I'd best toss a guilder," he told himself, producing a coin from his pocket, but he was just about to spin it when a voice hailed him.

"To the left, sir, if you please. Turn left and keep straight on, and you'll find what you seek."

Poker was startled. A dozen paces from him stood a man wearing a red jerkin and a waggoner's hat with a feather in it, and in his hand was a waggoner's whip.

"Where did you spring from, fellow?" Poker exclaimed in surprise. "Upon my soul, I neither saw nor heard you coming."

"The wind blew me down from a tree," the man in the red jerkin replied with a laugh, cracking his whip. "Don't you remember me?"

He came closer, and Poker looked into his face. It was yellow and as full of creases and wrinkles as an old glove, and his eyes were so sunken that they lent him an alarming appearance. Poker was unafraid, however. He would not have taken fright at Satan himself because he knew that man's cruelty to man was more to be feared than all the devils in hell.

"Yes, I remember you," he said. "You're the one the folk on the bishop's estate call 'the Dead Miller'. They say you're no mortal creature. They say you can walk the earth for one day only each year, and when that day is up you turn back into a little heap of dust and ashes. A dog could carry you off in its jaws, they say. Is today your day, if I may be permitted to ask?"

The man in the red jerkin bared his teeth in an angry grimace.

"Pay no heed to what the riff-raff say," he said. "They talk a great deal, but I find their babblings tedious and nonsensical. Remembering me as you do, you must know that I'm my lord bishop's waggoner. I've been on the road for a year. I come from Harlem and Liège, bringing my princely master damask napery and Brabant lace and tulip bulbs from Holland. You'll also remember, sir, that it was I –"

"Don't call me 'sir'," Poker broke in. "I'm no gentleman. My name and rank are gone with the wind."

"You'll also remember, sir," the man in the red jerkin went on, quite undeterred, "that it was I that set you on the road to an easy life."

"Yes, may the hangman reward you for it," Poker exclaimed. "An easy life, forsooth! A dozen strokes on the back before you've even touched your breakfast gruel, that's an easy life indeed!"

"Yes," said the man who claimed to be the bishop's waggoner, "his lordship's bailiff rules those rogues with a rod of iron, but how should it be otherwise? Justice must prevail. When a man has served his term honestly, however, he gets his just reward."

Poker's face darkened with anger.

165

"If you mean to annoy me, fellow," he cried, "have a care or I'll choke you! Six guilders and a half were all I got. The rest all went for bread and dripping and scraps of meat in the soup. The clerk struck them off in that godforsaken ledger of his."

"His lordship, too, has cares and concerns in these costly, difficult days," the man in the red jerkin said plaintively, pulling a long face. "Maintaining a princely household takes money, and where's it to come from? The taxes on meat and ale have been pledged long ago, so the bishop's demesne must pay. But you, sir, will not be the loser. Your dearest wishes will be granted before the day is out."

"Find yourself a fool elsewhere," Poker growled. "How would you know what I want?"

"You want a swift horse and a sword," said the man in the red jerkin.

"Yes, and a brace of pistols," Poker exclaimed in surprise, "but how the deuce did you know?"

"I read it in your eyes, sir," said the man who claimed to be a waggoner. "And I know something else: you mean to steal the horse from a farmer's stable."

"Damn you!" Poker shouted. "How dare you say such a thing? Do you take me for a rogue?" Then, when it struck him that the man with the crooked mouth and bared teeth was telling the truth, he added, "I only meant to borrow it."

"You must not burden your conscience needlessly, sir," said the man in the red jerkin. "Turn left and keep straight on until you see the windmill and the miller's house on the hill. Then go in and sit down. You need not trouble yourself further: the horse will be to hand, complete with saddle and harness."

"I think you a liar and an impostor, fellow, but no matter," said Poker. "I mean to see what lies behind your words." And he took the road that led to the mill.

The axle of the great crab could be heard creaking a long way off and the windmill's sails swooped and soared, but nothing else stirred, nor was there any living creature to be seen. Poker

166

looked for the promised horse in stable and paddock, but to no avail. "It serves you right for believing such a cock-and-bull story!" he told himself. Storm clouds were gathering in the sky, so he retired to the miller's house.

The parlour looked as if no one had set foot in it for many years. Cobwebs hung from the walls, the table and chairs, closet and chest were thickly coated with dust, and the broken shutters rattled in the wind. Poker looked about him for something to eat – he would have been content with a morsel of biscuit and a mug of wine – but all he found was an old, dog-eared pack of French playing cards. He tried to pass the time by playing a hand of piquet against himself, but he soon tired of it. He stretched out on the bench beside the stove, listened awhile to the crab creaking and the rain pattering down, and fell asleep.

He slept so soundly that he failed to wake up when the Swedish cavalier and Wryneck walked in with a jingle of spurs.

The Swedish cavalier, knowing that it could no longer be averted, had resigned himself to his fate. Now that he bore the brand-mark on his brow, the one place in the world still open to him was the bishop's inferno, last resort of those destined for the gallows. Wryneck, however, was in an evil temper and unable to grasp, even now, why things had turned out so badly for them. While sitting there and waiting for the landlord or the miller to come and inquire their pleasure, he heaped his former captain with reproaches.

"My advice was sound, but you wouldn't heed it. You could have become a general in the Swedish army – we'd have looted and plundered and made our fortunes. Look at you now! I haven't seen you in as sorry a state since that time in Magdeburg Gaol."

"Leave him be! You talk more nonsense in one breath than I in a year," called Veiland, who had remained outside in the paddock and was rubbing down the horses after their hard ride.

The Swedish cavalier dabbed his forehead with a piece of cloth soaked in oil. His thoughts had strayed. It was night-time, and he was in his daughter's bedchamber. Maria Christine slipped out of bed and put her arms around his neck. He could feel her heart beating. "You're here," she whispered, soft as a breeze. "You're here and I won't let you go." "But you must," he replied, soft as the patter of raindrops. "I'll come again, but I must rejoin the Swedish army. I have a horse that soars over hedges and stiles." "In seven hours five hundred miles," she whispered back.

He raised his head and the agreeable vision faded. The gibbet adorning his forehead could be seen in the clouded mirror on the wall above the closet.

"If only I could sink into eternal darkness and sleep for ever more," he muttered.

"And what's to become of us?" Wryneck demanded implacably. "We're no use to you now. Do you still have your arcanum, Captain? Much luck it brought us! Take the thing and throw it out of the window – maybe a passing peasant will trip over it and break his neck. Where the devil's that landlord? Why doesn't he show himself when guests are in the house?"

He rose and walked across the room. Then he caught sight of Poker stretched out on the bench beside the stove.

"I don't believe it!" he cried indignantly. "Here he is, fast asleep beside the stove. Wake up, fellow, you've got company. Bestir yourself and bring us something to drink!"

He kicked Poker hard in the ribs. Sleepily, Poker sat up. Fancying that he was still in the smeltery, and that the foreman had taken him by surprise, he struggled to his feet.

"Yes, it's time," he muttered. "Two hours are up and the furnace must be stoked."

"Stoked or not, we're here," cried Wryneck. "See to it that we get something to drink. We've waited long enough."

"At once, sir," Poker grunted, still half asleep. "Coal into the stokehole, coal and yet more coal. The flames must be white, with no sparks or smoke. And now the ore, two heaped basketfuls of it . . ."

Wryneck shook his head and turned to the Swedish cavalier.

"Can you understand him, Captain?" he asked. "I can't. I think he's possessed by evil spirits."

The Swedish cavalier glanced briefly at Poker's face.

"That's not the landlord," he said. "From the way he raves about furnaces, I'd guess him to be a fugitive from the bishop's inferno."

Poker had recovered his wits by now and knew where he was.

"Good evening, sirs," he said, rubbing his eyes.

"To hell with your good evening," growled Wryneck. "Where's the landlord? We've sat here for God alone knows how long, and haven't seen hide nor hair of him."

"I don't know where he is," Poker replied. "He promised me a saddle-horse because I've a long ride ahead of me, but he hasn't kept his word."

"If you don't have a horse, ride shanks's pony," snapped Wryneck, who was now a sworn enemy of the whole human race.

His sarcasm went unheeded. Poker was staring spellbound at the Swedish cavalier's blue tunic.

"Am I mistaken, or have I the honour to address an officer of the Swedish Crown?" he asked. "Do you come from the army, sir?"

"Directly so," said the Swedish cavalier, thinking the conversation closed.

"Are you wounded, sir?" asked Poker, pointing to the piece of cloth that hid the brand-mark.

"A mere scratch," the Swedish cavalier replied with a shrug, but Wryneck, who considered no lie too brazen to foist on such an unwelcome inquisitor, said, "Three or four Tatars tried to split his skull with their curved sabres."

"But he distinguished himself by fighting them off against all odds!" Poker exclaimed in high delight. "Yes indeed, a Swedish officer knows how to use his sword. Tell me, sir, do you bring news from headquarters? Has King Charles won another victory?"

"No," said the Swedish cavalier, overcome with rage

because this stranger persisted in pestering him with questions. "The Muscovites are driving our men before them on every front."

"Is it possible? Have things changed so much? How can it be?" Poker looked dismayed and dumbfounded. "What of General Lewenhaupt and Field Marshal Rehnskjöld?"

"They're at daggers drawn," the Swedish cavalier told him.

"But the rank and file?"

"They've long been sick to death of war. They yearn to go home to their fields, and their officers, too, have had enough of fighting."

"You must excuse me, sir, but I don't understand you," Poker said, looking angry and defiant. "Do you imply that the officers are reluctant to fight under a king before whom the whole world trembles?"

"No one trembles before him," the Swedish cavalier replied, coldly and sarcastically. 'What great feats has the king performed? He has ruined his country's finances with his childish escapades, nothing more – everyone in the Swedish army says so."

There was a brief silence. Then, in a calm, resolute voice, Poker said, "You lie, sir. You were never in the Swedish army."

"Wryneck," said the Swedish cavalier, turning to his servant, "I begin to find this fellow irksome. Get rid of him for me."

Wryneck strode up to Poker and gripped him by the arm.

"Come, fellow," he said. "For your health's sake, go and take the air outside. The rain has stopped."

With one effortless sweep of the arm, Poker sent Wryneck flying into a corner. Then he walked slowly over to the Swedish cavalier and confronted him, hands on hips.

"That was a lie," he said, "an infamous lie – and leave your sausage-spit in its scabbard or I'll break it in pieces for you! So you served with distinction in the Swedish army and were wounded in battle, were you? I wonder! Down where I come from, many of those that haul the carts are loath to show their foreheads. Let's see what badge of honour or shame *you* are hiding!"

Very swiftly, he reached out and tore the strip of cloth from the other man's head.

The Swedish cavalier jumped up and clapped a hand to the gibbet-mark, but it was too late. He let it fall.

And then, as they stood there in silence, face to face and eye to eye, recognition dawned.

"In Christ's name!" the Swedish cavalier exclaimed. "Is it you?"

"Can it really be you, friend?" cried the other, much moved. "How comes it that I find you here?"

"It's you, and I gave you up for dead!"

"And you, how did your life come to grief? What gaol do you come from? What galley?"

"Thank God you escaped the inferno, friend!"

"But did you not mean to join the Swedish army in my place?"

"It's a long story. I thought my fortunes would be better served at home. If you could only forgive me for what I did to you!"

"What did you do to me? I've been through hell and survived it – I'm hardened in the fire. But tell me, friend, how I can help you?"

"No one can help me. I'm bound for the bishop's inferno, where I shall hide myself away. And you, where are you off to?"

"The Swedish war. I mean to serve my king."

"You're ill provided for the journey."

"No matter, friend, I'll manage. Down there I learned to defy all the powers that be."

"I have a horse – you must take it. My sword, my pistols, my valise, my purse, my two servants – all are yours."

"That's more than I need. Keep your valise and your purse. How can I ever thank you? But what of the arcanum I entrusted to you – what of Gustavus Adolphus' bible?"

"Here it is, friend. Take it."

171

"Thank heavens I have it again – now I can give it to the king in person. And you, friend . . ."

"Is the bargain struck?" said a grating voice. "If so, you must seal it with a glass."

Behind them stood the miller in his red jerkin, a smile on his twisted lips and a glass of brandy wine in either hand.

Charles XII's new-found officer took one of the glasses and raised it.

"I drink to you, friend," he said. "May your courage survive the flames unscathed."

"And may you and your sword prevail," the other rejoined.

Then they took leave of each other.

The true Christian von Tornefeld rode off to the Swedish war with his two servants while a nameless man followed the miller into the bishop's hellish domain.

Rain beat down and wind lashed the treetops as they made their way through the forest by the light of the miller's lantern. His footsteps became ever slower. He stumbled over every stone, every root in his path, like one whose strength is ebbing away.

At last he paused beside a long, narrow hummock overgrown with tousled clumps of grass.

"You must go on alone," he told his companion. "You'll not lose your way now. Don't heed me, I'll stay here. This path is too much for me."

"But it's not the first time you've come this way," said the nameless man.

"First or last, it's too much for me – I can go no further," groaned the miller. He sank down on the hummock and set the lantern beside him. "Another hundred paces and you'll see flames darting from the smelting furnaces."

"Is that a grave?" asked the nameless man. "I see no cross."

"A man lies buried here in unconsecrated ground," said the miller, "a man who, one ill-starred night, placed a rope about his own neck. Let me tell you how it happened. As the noose drew tight he heard the wind howl, 'It's a sin! It's a sin!' but by then it was too late. An owl beat on the window with its wings and cried, 'The fire, the purifying fire!' but by then it was all over with him."

The miller's head sank on to his chest and his voice became no louder than the snap of a dry twig.

"When folk saw him hanging there," he went on, "they ran to the mayor, but he told them it was the hangman's business: the hangman must cut him down, he said, not the parish. The district magistrate, for his part, decreed that the parish must do it because the dead man had not been executed. So there he continued to hang until the mayor came and ordered some poor soul to cut him down. He was buried in the forest, no one in the village knows where."

The wind shook the trees, dislodging one shower of raindrops after another. The miller's huddled form subsided more and more.

"He lies here in the earth awaiting God's mercy," he whispered. "Now go your way. Walk on for the space of two Paternosters and you'll see the bishop's servants. They'll beat you – that's their custom – but you must endure it. Afterwards, tell them that I've repaid the last pfennig of my debt to the bishop, and that I shall never return."

The nameless man walked on through the forest for the space of two Paternosters, then paused and looked back. The lantern had gone out, and he could see neither the miller nor his grave. And then, as he continued on his way toward the darting flames, the bishop's servants emerged from the trees.

Among the miscreants who fled the Emperor's jurisdiction and sought refuge in the bishop's inferno there were some who, on finding the work too hard for them and the fare too meagre, had the temerity to rebel against their foremen and set upon them with their fists, or even with cudgels. Accordingly, it had become common practice for all newcomers to be fettered forthwith. The stone-breakers wore leg-irons, the men that hauled the carts were manacled, and thus they remained day and night, both at work and at rest, until their spirit was broken and they learned to submit to the harshest discipline.

The nameless man, who did his work without demur, had his irons removed after only two weeks. A few hours later he escaped.

Only one who held his life cheap could have performed such a feat. Work went on day and night in the stamp-mill and around the smelting furnaces and limekilns, so it was impossible to steal past them unobserved. In the west, however, where the quarries lay, the diocesan estate was bounded by a precipitous wall of rock some three or four hundred feet high. The guards felt satisfied that no one could scale this in darkness, but the nameless man ascended a vertical cleft by moonlight. He toiled upwards in peril of his life, step by step, until he derived some measure of safety from the fir trees that clung to the rock half-way up. Once at the top he granted himself a few minutes' rest. Then he hurried on, at first by way of remote forest paths and then along the highroad, hiding whenever anyone passed him. He reached Kleinroop Manor an hour after midnight.

He lurked among the bushes in the garden and waited till the old night watchman had gone his rounds, then knocked at the window of his daughter's bedchamber.

This was the moment for which he had risked his life and would have to risk it again before the night was out. When he cupped Maria Christine's face in his hands and a low cry of joy betokened that she had recognised him, the burden he bore by day was forgotten. The pangs of hunger, the heavy carts laden with stone, the rope that bit into his shoulder, the foremen's blows, the shouts and imprecations of his companions in misfortune – all these had ceased to matter.

Maria Christine had much to ask and even more to tell.

"Have you come far? You're tired, I expect. Where's your horse? Where are the servants who rode with you? Had you come yesterday you would have seen me riding too – on the chestnut mare, twice up and down the stable yard, and I wasn't frightened. There was a fair in the village. It was very droll. I wanted to dance too, but Mother wouldn't let me. 'Your father's away at the war,' she said. 'Do you know what it is, a war?' And I said I knew very well. A war is when the flags flutter and the drums go boom-boom-boom."

He could not linger, having so far to go, though Maria Christine wept when he bade her adieu.

Early next morning, when the quarry foreman blew his bugle to signify that the day's work had begun, the nameless man was ready and waiting beside his cart.

Three days went by before he tapped on the window at the same hour. Maria Christine, who had feared that he wouldn't come again, gave a little exclamation of surprise and delight.

"Mother said I must have dreamt it," she whispered. "People often visit you at night who cannot be seen by day, she told me. Grandfather and Grandmother went to heaven a long time ago, so if they come at night it's a dream. Are you in heaven?"

"No," the nameless man replied, "I'm here on earth. I'm alive."

"Then why don't you come in the daytime?"

"Because my horse travels too slowly by day. At night it soars over hedges and stiles, in one little hour five hundred miles."

Maria Christine nodded vigorously. It pleased her that his horse should fly through the air so fast, and besides, the words had a familiar ring.

"When Herod's palace came in sight," she sang in her piping voice, "the king looked down and shone a light . . . The first time you came I thought it was Herod and didn't want to see him. Why do you keep your hat pulled down so low? *Are* you Herod?"

"No. You know very well who I am."

"Yes, I know it so I'm not afraid – I know you by your voice. And tomorrow, if Mother tells me again I was dreaming –"

"You were dreaming," the nameless man said quietly but firmly.

175

Maria Christine fell silent. Something told her that she must keep her father's furtive comings and goings to herself.

The nameless man kissed her on the brow and eyelids.

"Where's your horse?" she asked.

"Not far away," the nameless man replied. "Listen hard and you'll hear it snorting in the darkness." Then he disappeared among the alder bushes.

He came again. The third time he escaped from the bishop's inferno his ascent of the cliff seemed easy and devoid of danger. He saw as he crossed his fields to the manor house – it no longer seemed so far to come – that the wheat and oats were thriving, and that the plough and harrow had done their work well.

He returned many times, his nocturnal conversations with Maria Christine being his one remaining solace in life. The thought that he would never see his wife again was hard to endure, but he forced himself not to dwell on it. As a branded slave in the bishop's inferno, he could have no beloved wife. The child was all he had.

Meanwhile, word had come from the Swedish army that Christian von Tornefeld's star was in the ascendant. The couriers who changed horses at Kleinroop had at first shaken their heads or shrugged their shoulders when Maria Agneta inquired after Herr von Tornefeld, who had joined the army with two servants; his name was unknown to them. After some weeks, however, they all had something new to report:

"Tornefeld? An officer of that name has lately distinguished himself on patrol."

"If you mean Lieutenant Tornefeld of the Westgöta Cavalry, he acquitted himself so bravely at Yeresno, while our forces were crossing the river under enemy fire, that his colonel shook him by the hand in front of all his brother officers when the battle was over."

"He was privileged to present His Majesty with a book, reputedly a bible from the time of Gustavus Adolphus."

"Who hasn't heard of Tornefeld?" a courier exclaimed two

weeks later. "With only a handful of men, he captured four field guns and their limbers at Baturin."

And again, after another few days:

"His Majesty has promoted him captain of cavalry."

These tidings filled Maria Agneta with pride and joy, and also with a certain measure of confidence in the future. After so many victories and such great feats of arms, she told herself, peace could not be long in coming; and when word arrived that the Swedes had won another victory at Gorskva, and that Christian von Tornefeld, now colonel of the Småland Dragoons, had that evening been publicly kissed on both cheeks by His Majesty, she felt that the war was as good as over. The Muscovites would never risk another encounter with the Swedish army, and she would soon see her Christian once more.

Then came a period of time when the couriers had little to report. The Swedish army lay encamped before the palisades of Poltava.

One night in late July, the nameless man caught sight of his wife.

He had spoken with his daughter, as so often before, and was about to steal away through the garden when he heard a noise. He crouched and froze. An upstairs window opened and Maria Agneta leaned out.

He stood motionless among the alder bushes, not daring to breathe, but his heart pounded fit to burst. She must surely see him, he thought, but she did not; she looked up at the clouds drifting across the sky and drew in deep breaths of night air with the moonlight flowing over her hair and shoulders like molten silver. The garden was hushed. All that could be heard was the chirp of a belated cricket and the rustle of a bird in the leaves overhead.

The window closed, the vision vanished. The nameless man stood there spellbound for a full minute, gazing up at the house. Then he fled.

He fled from his own tempestuous thoughts, but they gave

him no peace. He wrestled with them all day as he breathlessly hauled the cart from the quarry to the limekilns and from there to the quarry again. He was in a turmoil. She had been so close to him! Nothing would banish her nocturnal image from his mind's eye.

Hadn't she loved him and lived with him for seven long years? Mightn't that love be strong enough to forgive what he had done in order to win her? He had deceived her and lied to her, but if he now told her everything – if he told her how it had all begun and how his blissful contentment had ended in utter misery – mightn't he hope for forgiveness and a word of consolation? But if she shrank from the brand-mark on his brow – if she condemned and rejected him, what then?

In his bewildered state, he knew only one thing for certain: he could endure his present way of li.. no longer.

By nightfall his mind was made up: he would go to her, reveal himself to her in all his wretchedness, and open his heart. He would tell her all that he had concealed from her for seven years.

But it was not to be: fate decreed otherwise.

That night, while he was scaling the cliff, a stone gave way beneath him. He slipped, clung there for an instant, and plunged into the abyss.

He lay at the foot of the cliff with shattered limbs, unable to cry out, unable to move. It hurt him even to breathe.

Toward midnight a guard came by with a lantern and saw him lying there.

"Where did you spring from?" he asked. "What happened to you?"

The nameless man pointed to the cliff.

"You mean you were trying to escape?" said the guard. "You see? You should have known better."

He shone his lantern on the nameless man's face. Seeing the bluish pallor of impending death on his cheeks and lips, he put the lantern down beside him.

"Stay there, don't move. I'll fetch the surgeon."

The nameless man knew that he was dying. He had but one

wish, one thought, but it filled him to the brim: Maria Christine must be told of his death. She must not think that her father, when he failed to return, had forgotten her, and she must say a Paternoster for his soul.

"Not the surgeon," he whispered. "A priest."

Footsteps receded, other footsteps approached. He opened his eyes and saw a man in a brown habit bending over him.

"Father," he groaned, trying to raise himself a little, "there's an old boil of evil deeds in my heart. The time has come to lance it. I wish to confess my sins."

"Yes, Captain," replied a voice he knew. "There you lie with your limbs crushed by rocks like St Stephen himself. You're dying, Captain, so resign yourself."

The nameless man sank back and closed his eyes. It was his old comrade Feuerbaum that had come to confess him.

"Bid farewell to this world," the renegade friar intoned. "The world is mere outward show and its pleasures are worthless. Renounce your wealth, too. What use is your money now? You cannot take it with you into eternity."

The nameless man knew that he would have to die unshriven, for Feuerbaum wanted one thing of him only: he was eager to know where his erstwhile captain had hidden his share of guilders and ducats.

"Beware the flames of hell, Captain," Feuerbaum urged. "Be less stubborn and stiff-necked or they'll engulf you. Your money can avail you nothing, but it could be of help to many another. Give it up, and your soul will soar heavenwards like the lark at daybreak."

The nameless man's breath rattled in his throat.

"Why not play a trick on the Devil?" Feuerbaum suggested. "End your life with a good deed. If you tell me where you hid your money, you'll cheat the Devil and God will welcome you with open arms."

The nameless man said nothing.

"Go to hell, then," Feuerbaum shouted angrily, "and may ten thousand devils tussle over your soul!"

But the nameless man was listening no longer. Another

familiar figure now stood silent and motionless before him: the angelic swordbearer who had once accused him thrice in the cloudy vault of heaven.

"So it's you," the nameless man said without moving his lips. "Listen to me. I have often pondered on the divine court of justice, but it defied my comprehension. I think I understand it at last. You prayed for me once. Do so again now. My one desire is that my little daughter shall not believe, when I fail to return, that I have forgotten her. Let her be told that I am dead. She must not weep for me – I do not wish it – but let her say a Paternoster for my soul."

The angel of death looked up at the stars and stood there like a shadow. Then, in mute accord, he inclined his noble head.

At noon the next day, news of the battle at Poltava was brought to Kleinroop by a Swedish officer with his arm in a sling. The Swedish army had been annihilated, he said. The king had fled, and among the dead was that pride and glory of the Swedish army, Colonel Christian von Tornefeld.

Maria Agneta stood there in frozen-faced silence. At first she could not grasp what had happened. When she did, she was too overwhelmed with grief to weep. It was not until she reached her bedchamber that the tears began to gush from her eyes.

Toward evening she sent for her daughter. When Maria Christine came, she took her in her arms and covered her face with kisses.

"Child," she said in a low voice, "you will never see your father again. He has fallen in battle – they buried him three weeks since. You must join your hands and say a Paternoster for his soul."

Maria Christine looked at her and shook her head. She couldn't, wouldn't believe it.

"He'll return," she said.

Maria Agneta's eyes filled anew with tears.

"No," she said sadly, "he'll never return – never, don't you understand? He's in heaven. Join your hands and do your filial duty. He loved you just as I do, my treasure. And now, say a Paternoster for his soul."

Maria Christine was about to shake her head again when she caught sight of something on the highroad: a cart with a coffin on it was approaching from the direction of the bishop's estate. She clasped her hands together and bowed her head, and her lips moved in an unspoken prayer:

"Our Father which art in heaven, hallowed be Thy name, Thy kingdom come, Thy will be done . . . I'm praying for that poor man in the coffin there. There's no one to weep for him, may his soul rest in peace . . . And lead us not into temptation, but deliver us from evil, for Thine is the kingdom, the power, and the glory, for ever and ever. Amen."

Slowly, very slowly, the cart that was carrying the nameless man to his grave passed the window and disappeared from view.